BLOOD & VOWS

TWISTED LEGENDS COLLECTION

K. EASTON

Blood & Vows
Amanda Richardson Writing As K. Easton
Published by K. Easton
© Copyright 2022 Amanda Richardson/K. Easton
www.authoramandarichardson.com

Editing by Heart Full of Reads
Cover Design by Raven Designs

This is a work of fiction. Names, characters, businesses, places, events and incidents are either the products of the author's imagination or used in a fictitious manner. Any resemblance to actual persons, living or dead, or actual events is purely coincidental.

All rights reserved. This book or any portion thereof may not be reproduced or used in any manner whatsoever without the express written permission of the author except for the use of brief quotations in a book review.

Blurb

Never make a deal with the devil—especially if that deal entails holy matrimony.

There's only one rule my mother passed down to me before she died: Never venture into the east side of Edinburgh.
I never questioned it.

There are creatures in this world that could hurt us, she'd said.

So, I stay away—until my life hits rock bottom, and I find myself curious about the forbidden

side of the ancient city.
It doesn't seem all that different here–bars,
clubs, restaurants. Just like the human side.
One too many drinks later, he finds me.
A silly poem and a whispered wish are all
it takes for him to rip through the mirror
between realms and pin me against a wall.

Cruel, inhuman, cunning. A demon—an actual
prince from hell. *With horns.*
What could he possibly want from me?
Marriage, apparently.
Because as it turns out, Bloody Marius is dead
serious about upholding his end of the deal.

**Blood & Vows is a dark retelling of the
legend of Bloody Mary. It is a paranormal
romance with forced marriage themes.
Please note that this book is dark and can be
triggering for some.**

Dedication

For anyone who spent their childhood terrified of turning the bathroom light off and looking into the mirror…

Welcome...

*Ten authors invite you to join us in the
Twisted Legends Collection.*

These stories are a dark, twisted reimagining of infamous legends well-known throughout the world. Some are retellings, others are nods to those stories that cause a chill to run down your spine.

Each book may be a standalone, but they're all connected by the lure of a legend.

We invite you to venture into the unknown, and delve into the darkness with us, one book at a time.

TWISTED LEGENDS

AUTHOR SERIES

The COLLECTION

Vengeance of The Fallen - Dani René

Truth or Kill - A.C. Kramer

Departed Whispers - J Rose

The Labyrinth of Savage Shadows - Murphy Wallace

Hell Gate - Veronica Eden

Blood & Vows - Amanda Richardson

Under the Cover of Darkness - Emma Luna

Reckless Covenant - Lilith Roman

Bane & Bound - Crimson Syn

The Ripper - Alexandra Silva

One
LIZ

I KNOW WHERE I'M GOING THE INSTANT I LEAVE MY house. The autumn air is crisp, making my skin pucker with goosebumps. Dark clouds hang over the stone city I call home, and I pull my wool coat tighter as my sneakers slam against the pavement. I know where I'm going, because I'm finally desperate enough to put my life in danger. Finally numb enough to yearn for something dangerous, something to make me feel again.

When your life implodes, you stop caring about the things that once gave you nightmares.

Edinburgh is busy tonight. The tourists are

out in full swing, their phones out at every corner, taking pictures of the winding, cobblestone streets and famous cafés. I don't mind it. The hordes of people make me feel a little less alone. Still, the ache of what happened sears through my heart again when I think about it—and the people who betrayed me.

And the betrayal happened just a week after losing my job.

It's like the world conspired to make me feel as miserable as possible, ensuring I had no respite, no time to catch my breath before one tragedy turned into three.

My phone chimes, and when I look down, I see Shepherd's name flash across the screen. After hitting the ignore button, I hold the power button down and wait for my phone to go black. The only two people who would ever need to get a hold of me just decided to stab me in the back, so there's no need to keep it powered on. If a bus were to hit me now, no one would know, because they wouldn't realize that I'm missing. That thought depresses me even more, and I swallow the lump in my throat as I nearly collide with someone, deep in thought. I swallow and rub my neck, shaking my head.

It's fine. I am better off alone.

I turn down Princes Street, walking past the shops and restaurants I know like the back of my hand. Making a sharp left, I head down a narrow, unnamed alleyway. It's one of the secret veins of the city—a passage between the human territory and the *other* territory. Growing up, I was told not to venture east, not to enter this passage. But tonight, I can't seem to find the energy to care. I just need a space away from my memories, somewhere new.

Somewhere Shepherd and Rachel won't find me.

A few minutes later, I emerge on the other side. I don't know what I expected. My mother told me horror stories my entire childhood, warned me of the beasts that roamed freely here, thanks to an old, Scottish law. This was the one section of Edinburgh that belonged to them. Two streets—that's it. As I look around, all I see are… humans. Bars, restaurants, shops, people walking and talking… It's exactly like every other part of the city. There are fewer tourists, sure, but there are no winged faeries or fanged vampires roaming around unchecked.

I pick the first bar I see. Dante's Inferno.

Ha, ha, ha.

My lips quirk at the irony, but my smile drops off my face the second I enter the disheveled bar. A group of frumpy, older women sit in one corner, and a few couples are scattered around the bar. Why was my mother so adamant that I stay away from this area? It doesn't seem any different, and as far as I can tell, everyone is purely human. Disappointed, I take a seat at the bar and get the bartender's attention. He's tall and thin with blue eyes; older, perhaps mid-forties. His silver hair is shiny and neat. I study his face for any clues, but to me, he looks just like every other human.

"Hello, what can I get you?" he chirps, sauntering over to me.

"Your strongest drink?" I ask. I'm usually a wine or beer girl, but tonight, I need something stronger. Shrugging off my coat, I take a seat at the bar.

"Rough day?"

"Something like that," I respond.

His eyebrows knit together, and he pouts. "Do you like whiskey?"

I wrinkle my nose. "Not usually."

"Even quadruple distilled whiskey? It's 96 proof, made in-house. The recipe is from the sixteenth century," he adds, his voice high and excited. "One drink of the stuff and you won't remember whoever is making you so sad."

I grin. "That sounds perfect."

He smiles as he reaches for an old bottle with a wax cap. Pouring me a finger in a crystal glass, he sets it down in front of me.

"Best drunk straight," he adds, his Scottish accent thick.

I'm used to the accents now. I moved back and forth between Edinburgh and New York my entire childhood, so I'm an expert at picking up mumbled Scottish terms and phrases.

Taking a sip of the amber liquid, I blink a few times to disguise the fact that the strength burns my throat and makes my eyes water. The bartender chuckles, and I set the glass down.

"Careful with that one," he continues, polishing a glass a few feet away. "One glass and you won't remember tonight."

I tilt my head and lift the glass, giving him a little smile as I shoot the rest of the drink.

Holy gods, it burns.

I cough a couple of times, hitting my chest and squeezing my eyes shut. "Fuck," I whisper, shaking my head.

"Told you." The bartender chuckles.

"Another one," I manage to get out, sliding the glass over to him.

"Who hurt you?" he jokes, pulling the bottle down from the shelf again and refilling my glass.

"Is that question rhetorical?"

He slides the glass back. "It doesn't have to be."

I hum in response. My mouth and throat are numb, and I lift the second glass to my lips, shooting that one back as well.

"Well, my dad left my mom when I was a baby. That's probably where my issues started, when I think about it." I move my hand in circles next to my head. "*Major* daddy issues. Anyway, my mom was my best friend, and I had to watch her die slowly from early onset Alzheimer's five years ago. My boyfriend at the time was my only bright spot. Soon after, I met my best friend, Rachel. And about two hours ago, I caught them cheating on me. With each other." My lower lip wobbles, and I sniff as I take a deep breath. "Shepherd and I were together for six years."

The bartender lowers himself so that he's at eye-level with me, his elbows resting on the bar. "Your ex sounds like a fucking twat," he says softly.

I look up at him through wet lashes. His face is so sincere. My eyes prick with tears because of it. Swooping a gaze over his face, I see that his nails are hot pink, and he's wearing a rainbow lanyard around his neck. I give him a small smile before pushing my empty glass back. Feeling dizzy, I shake my head.

"To make matters worse, I got fired from my job earlier this week. So, I'm truly and utterly alone," I explain, throat stinging. "Hence the whiskey. I think I'll take another glass," I add, gripping the edge of the bar.

"You can get another job," he answers, his voice resolved. "There are plenty of jobs out there. And fuck your ex and your friend. You don't need them." He sighs. "This is going to sound harsh, but I promise you need to hear it.

If they truly cared about you, they would've put you first. Instead, two awful people found each other. Think about it that way."

I shrug. "I just wish it wasn't the two people I cared about the most."

The bartender smirks. "How big was his cock?"

I huff a laugh. "It was… average?"

He shakes his head. "No. You and me? We need big dick energy, you hear me?"

I laugh, and he slides another drink over to me. I shoot it back easier this time because my throat has lost all feeling.

"I just wish I could forget about them, you know?" I admit, feeling vulnerable.

The bartender nods, and I swear his eyes flash a brighter blue for a second. "Trust me. My ex takes up way too much space in my mind. His cock wasn't even that big," he adds. "Big dick energy was lacking, aye." I laugh, feeling a tiny bit better. "What's your name?" he asks, setting down a glass of water.

"Elizabeth, but everyone calls me Liz."

He twists his lips. "Okay, Liz. Here's what you're going to do. You're going to drink that water, eat a proper meal, and get some sleep. Tomorrow, when you're sober, you're going to come back here and ask my manager for a job. Tell him Rory sent you."

Maybe it's the alcohol, or maybe it's just the events of the day catching up with me, but I blurt out the first thought that pops into my mind. I mean it to sound funny, like a joke—and if this place is truly paranormal, perhaps this is the way to put feelers out.

"Even though I'm human?"

Rory's eyes flash again, and his eyebrows rise just a fraction. "Pardon?"

I giggle, feeling rubbery and loose. "My mom told me this part of Edinburgh was inhabited with demons, faeries, and werewolves," I explain, my voice a little too loud. The bar quiets, and Rory looks around before bending forward.

"I think you've had a bit too much to drink, Liz," he whispers. "The drinks are on me. Why don't you go home and come back tomorrow?"

His brush-off stings a bit, but I'm too tipsy to care. "Sure. Can I use the restroom?"

He points behind me. "It's downstairs, to

the right."

Nodding, I hop off the stool and stumble, catching myself on a nearby chair before I fall on my ass. I hear Rory curse under his breath, so I straighten and brush myself off. The room spins around me. He wasn't lying when he said the whiskey would do me in. Heading in the direction Rory pointed to, I see a stone staircase leading down to the basement. I take the steps one at a time, holding onto the railing for dear life. Despite feeling drunk, I also feel… happy. Numb. Maybe this is why people drink whiskey. The staircase winds down and down, and my thighs are burning just before my feet find solid ground.

It's like a dungeon in here, not unlike the vaults I frequented for my job. I look around, turning right and facing a door with a toilet sign. But to my left is a dark passageway, and perhaps my only clue to what the hell my mother was so scared of. I trudge on, slowly walking into the darkness. It's cold down here, and the skin on my bare arms prickles with goosebumps. I pull my phone out of my back pocket and clumsily turn on the flashlight, holding it out in front of me. The only sound I hear is my own breathing, so I continue for another minute, until I reach a dead end. Looking around, my eyes dart around the stone chamber, but there's nothing down here.

This place is no different from any other old bar I've been to. What the hell was my mom talking about when she warned me of this place as a child?

I turn around and head to the toilet. It's a large bathroom, with a curved, stone ceiling and gothic furniture. I lock the door and use the toilet. When I'm done, I walk up to the ornate, wooden vanity, and wash my hands. I stare at my reflection in the mirror. My long, red hair is up in a bun, though it's messier now than it was a few hours ago. And my light brown eyes are glossed over, the whiskey making it so that I can barely focus on my own reflection. I'm about to turn around when my eyes catch a small piece of paper next to the mirror—scrawled handwriting on an old piece of parchment, framed behind a pane of glass. I lean forward to read it.

In the mirror, his soul now rests,
Speak your wish, name your test,

To pass the time, he opens this gate,
Bloody Marius is cursed to wait.
A sacrifice is all he asks,
For even the most disagreeable tasks,
Look through the mirror and speak into,
Just be warned, he might choose you.

I rear my head back and repeat the poem out loud. As I finish reciting it, the lights in the bathroom flicker, and the hair stands up on the back of my neck as the bathroom goes dark. I should run, but the whiskey running through my veins gives me faux courage. *A wish?* I can speak my wish to whatever the hell is behind this mirror. Fuck it.

I huff a laugh and lean forward on the vanity so that my nose is touching the mirror. I expect to bite out a snarky wish, but the events of the day catch up with me, and my chest begins to ache when I think of what happened.

Shepherd screwing Rachel in our flat.

Having to face them in the future—*watch* them together.

Not having my mom or dad or anyone I can confide in.

Not going to university so that I could stay

near Shepherd.

After my mom died, he was all I had after all.

And here I am, in the bathroom of a bar on the *other* side of town.

The one place my mother asked me to stay away from.

But why did she want me to stay away so badly? She left so many questions unanswered, because her mind was all over the place at the end.

And now, tonight, I am all alone.

Tonight, I have a death wish, because there is no one left to care about what happens to me.

The weight of that loneliness settles deep in my bones, and my head drops as I stare at the black marble sink.

"I wish I had someone to worry about me," I whisper, tears falling from my eyes.

My vision is blurry when I look up at myself in the mirror.

Except… it's not my reflection staring back.

It's a man—and his eyes are just as wide as mine. His face is young yet weathered—not old, but somehow wise. *Powerful.* His eyes glow red, and his hair is black and combed back, like he's from another era. His stiff collar has gold buttons, and his red coat matches the color of his eyes.

Dread fills every crevice, every molecule of my body. I'm dreaming. I passed out somewhere, and I'm dreaming. I must be. Before I can fully register what's happening, like an apparition, he *steps* through the mirror. I stumble backward as he appears in front of me—a fully-fledged person, flesh and bone and skin. He's wearing black trousers and a red overcoat. Not a reflection—a *man*. A very tall, very menacing-looking man. *With horns.* My eyes widen at the black horns sticking out of the top of his head, and when my eyes find his red ones again, I open my mouth to scream.

He rushes forward with otherworldly speed and cups my mouth with his hand. His skin is cold, too cold. He's a solid foot taller than me, and he overpowers me easily. Bending down, his hot breath tickles my ear, sending shivers down my body and something else, some sort of power that relaxes me instantly.

"I've been waiting a long, long time for you,

Elizabeth," he growls.

My vision tilts a bit before everything goes black.

Two
MARIUS

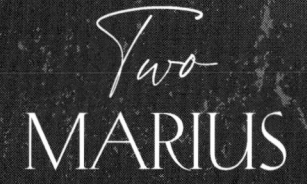

Five minutes ago

I SHOOT OUT OF MY SEAT AND GRAB MY COAT, THE FURY inside of my veins building with each second that passes. Throwing my coat on, I storm to my bedroom door and throw it open so hard that the marble wall cracks. I don't care; I don't give a fuck about anything except getting to *her*. My valet rushes over to me, but I don't have time to explain. Every cell in my body throbs in tandem with hers. My blood warms and my heart races. I know exactly where she is. I heard her call my name. The glamour is off, and she is *mine*.

"Sir?" Charles asks, trotting behind me as I

stalk to the staircase.

I hardly hear him. Using a bit of my speed power, the stairs blur as I rush down and down and down, until I'm in the basement. Just as I predicted, the large mirror propped up on the dresser is smoking, and my eyes scan hers just as she finishes reciting that stupid fucking poem Rory insists on hanging up. He's always been a bit theatrical. Growling, I stare at her reflection, my anger burning so hot that it burns the wood beneath my palms.

I can smell her, even from here. More specifically, I can smell the blood that runs through her veins, because it's mine. *She* is mine. The lights behind her flicker, and I take in her young face just as everything goes dark. A low snarl escapes my lips, and her eyes snap to mine. My heart pounds as she locks eyes with me. Red hair, just like her mother. Her large eyes are the color of honey, and her face... she looks so different from the last time I saw her. The beast inside of me is pleased—pleased that she's nice to look at, which is convenient if we're to spend an eternity together.

I cock my head slightly as her chest heaves up and down, and my body moves forward before I can stop it. When I step through the mirror, I'm blanketed by her overpowering scent. I'd know that scent anywhere—cinnamon and honey. The same smell that haunts my dreams. The smell that caused me to rip through different realms to find her. The smell I've been waiting eighteen years to find.

Her eyes widen, and she opens her pretty little mouth to scream.

But I'm faster.

Rushing forward, I cup her mouth with my hand and bend down, slowly sniffing her hair, her neck. She's smaller than I expected her to be, vulnerable somehow…

I squeeze my eyes shut as my lips graze her ear.

Gods, I could stay here forever.

She trembles beneath my touch, so I send some soothing power through her. It's easy to do, seeing as our blood is linked. Relaxing instantly, she slumps against me slightly. I pull her closer, growling the only thing I can think of for such a pivotal moment.

"I've been waiting a long, long time for you, Elizabeth."

Three
LIZ

My head throbs as my eyes flutter open, and I throw an arm over my eyes as I sit up quickly.

"Whoa there," a man says, and I feel a cool hand against my forehead.

My eyes shoot open, and I wince. Rory the bartender is kneeling next to me. I'm still on the floor in the bathroom, and the light is on. I look around, trying to remember what happened and why I'm on the floor. My eyes catch on movement near the door, and my whole body stills when I spot *him* leaning against the doorframe.

"You must've passed out," Rory says, his voice concerned. He looks at the man standing by the door—the one now wearing jeans and a hoodie. No horns. No red eyes. Just a regular guy who is watching me with a grumpy expression and furrowed brows. "Marius, can you grab her some water?" Rory asks the man.

Marius...

Bloody Marius is cursed to wait...

Marius hesitates for a second, and then he's gone, leaving Rory and me alone. Rory helps me up and sits me down on the bench near the sink, near the mirror.

I groan. "I had the weirdest dream," I murmur. Pointing to the note, I let out a garbled laugh. "I read that poem, and that man appeared, except he was wearing this weird, red overcoat, and he had horns and red eyes—" I stop talking when I notice Rory smiling at me. "What?"

"I had no idea you were fae," he says softly. "If I'd known, I wouldn't have given you that human whiskey. I could've given you the fae—"

"No," I interrupt. I close my eyes and shake my head. "Hold on, what do you mean by *fae*?"

When I open my eyes, Rory's face is pinched

with concern. "You... don't know?"

"Rory."

The voice booms through the bathroom.

Rory and I look over at Marius, who is holding a glass of water. He walks over and sets it down next to me on the vanity.

"She doesn't know?" Rory asks, looking between us. Marius just scowls from his place by the door. "I thought you would've told her about the—"

"Oh my god, will one of you please just tell me what's going on?" I yell, and Rory stops talking, looking affronted.

"Marius. Your blood. The blood pact. The marriage." My eyes widen at the words Rory is throwing my way. "Your mother?" he asks.

I rear my head back. "What the fuck does my mother have to do with anything?"

"She glamoured you," Marius says, his voice gruff. "You're half-fae. When you summoned me in that mirror, it broke the glamour." He glowers at me, his brows furrowed. His accent is older and more ancient than Scottish. Latin, maybe? "Finally."

I look between them, unsure if I should

laugh or cry. Luckily, Rory interjects.

"We're fae, Liz. You, me, and most of the people in here."

I narrow my eyes. "What was all that stuff about blood and marriage and—"

"In exchange for saving your life nearly twenty years ago, your mother promised me your hand in marriage," Marius explains.

My stomach rolls with nausea. His words spin around in my head, but the whiskey and the fall make it so that I'm unable to process what he's saying. It doesn't make sense. Saving my life? My mother? There must be some weird fae-demon mix-up happening. I'm not fae, my mom didn't glamour me, and I'm sure as fuck not going to marry the dude with glowing, red eyes, and horns.

I've had enough of whatever the fuck is happening tonight.

"Okay, now I know I've had too much to drink," I say quickly, getting off the vanity and standing.

"You feel fine now, right?" Rory asks, smirking at me. I don't answer, and he smiles, crossing his arms. "It's because the glamour came off, Liz. Your fae blood is running wild in your veins—"

"*Half* fae blood," Marius growls from the corner.

I snap my heated gaze to Marius. He's just standing in the corner, like he's impatiently waiting for me to come to my senses or something.

"Is this some kind of joke?"

"It's not a joke," Marius says slowly, an angry bite to his words. "She hid you from me. She didn't keep her end of the bargain. But now that you're here, I'm not letting you go." He takes a menacing step forward. My skin crawls, and I bare my teeth at him.

"Like hell I am," I retort, my eyes darting to the door. Marius is blocking it, so I look to Rory. "I'm not marrying him. This is so fucking absurd. Let me go," I say with conviction before pushing past Rory. He grabs my arm, but I twist around and shove him off.

I smell the burning fabric before I see it.

My eyes slide down to his chest, and on his shirt is a hand mark—a black, charred hand mark. My eyes snap to my hand, and then they rove over to where Marius is watching me with red-tinged eyes. They're not as bright as before, but the outer irises are glowing.

"When your mother begged me to save your life, I used some of my blood to heal you," Marius says slowly, his eyes going back to a normal, golden color. His lips form a thin line, and the lines in his forehead make him seem like he's perpetually frowning. "Even as a baby, you knew what I was. And you took more than I wanted to give," he says slowly, his eyes flashing red with anger. "Your mother promised your hand in marriage, and then she glamoured you to cover the scent of my blood, and to cover the fact that you were half-fae," he spits.

I take a step back as he steps forward, crossing his arms. "I tore the world apart looking for you, Elizabeth. So, imagine my surprise when my name on your lips broke the glamour, and I knew exactly where you were after eighteen years."

"She would never do that," I hiss. "You didn't know her—"

"I did," he says. "You had a heart condition. It was fatal. But your mother loved you, and she knew of this place, of *me. In the mirror, his soul now rests. Speak your wish, name your test,*" he adds, reciting the poem. My skin pebbles. "So, when I offered to save you, to *heal* you with my blood, the only bargaining chip she had was... you." He cocks his head. "She thought she was so smart. Using her fae power to put a glamour on you. It was strong; I'll admit. But it wasn't strong enough."

Hot tears prick at my eyes. "You're lying."

His eyes lower to my neck, my chest. "If you don't believe me, can you tell me about the scar running down the middle of your chest?

My hand flies up to my neck, roving down between my breasts, along the jagged, bumpy scar. I can feel my heart racing against my rib cage on my sweaty palm.

"That was from falling through a glass table as a toddler," I answer, my voice wobbly. "I remember going to the hospital." Looking at Rory, he shakes his head. Even as the words clang around the empty bathroom, I realize they're not true. I never fell through glass. My vision blurs as tears pool in the corners of my eyes. I never understood why she was so adamant about me not roaming around this part of Edinburgh. "She knew you'd find me if I came here," I say quietly. "It's why she warned me to stay away."

"Saying his name broke the glamour," Rory says with awed conviction. "Oh, this is the most exciting thing that's ever happened to me," he squeals. Looking at me, he shrugs. "What? Even as a fae, life can get boring."

My jaw grinds as my fists open and close at my side. "I don't care what my mother promised. I'm not going with you," I tell Marius.

His golden eyes glow. "I'm not asking you. I'm telling you."

"Fuck off," I bite out, but it doesn't faze him.

"You have my blood, Elizabeth. I can command you to do whatever the fuck I want you to do."

My mouth opens and closes, and I look again to Rory, who looks as though he's watching a movie. I widen my eyes, pleading for him to save me.

"Oh," he says softly. "Sorry, sweetheart. I can't do anything against a blood bond. It's legally binding. But I promise you, Marius here is a good guy. And he definitely has big dick energy," he says, winking. A second later, he disappears. Just...*vanishes.*

I slowly turn to face Marius. "I'm not going with you," I say, my voice haughty.

Marius snaps his fingers, and the next thing I know, I'm being forced to my knees against my will. Some sort of power thrums through my veins, and even though I'm fully conscious, it's like my body is numb—like someone administered anesthesia, and my whole body is moving, able to be controlled by some outside force.

"What the fuck," I yelp, but then Marius cocks his head and my mouth snaps closed.

"I'm going to give you one chance to cooperate, Elizabeth," Marius purrs, circling me as I kneel before him. He rubs his lips, and a piece of dark hair falls in front of his forehead. "Either you can follow me of your own volition, or I can force you. The choice is yours." I try to whine, but nothing except a strangled garble comes out. He continues. "Whether you believe it or not, you now possess enough power to wipe out entire cities," he says, a bitter edge to his voice. "On your own, you are formidable. But together? We can rule the *world*."

He releases the hold of power on my throat, and I gasp for air as my chest heaves up and down. "I don't want to rule the world," I bark.

He rubs the back of his neck before stopping right in front of me. I peer up at him. "I don't think you understand," he murmurs. "You are twenty-two years old. You are an untrained fae. Yes, you have power, but you do not know how to wield it. Other people do, however. It would take one second for a creature with bad intentions to siphon your power. Remember what I said about wiping out entire cities? Imagine someone using your power for harm."

"And you won't?"

His face shutters for a second before resuming his grumpy demeanor. "Of course not."

I scoff. "I'm sure that's what they all say."

Marius huffs a laugh, but he doesn't smile. Instead, he drops to his knees in front of me. He's close enough that I can smell his musky, smokey scent, can see the flecks of what look like actual gold in his irises, framed by thick, black lashes. His skin is golden, his eyebrows arched and perfectly groomed. He's beautiful—there's no doubt about that. But it doesn't change the fact that he's kidnapping me against my will.

"I am the King of the Underworld, darling. If I wanted to use your power to control the world, I would have done it already."

I freeze. "You're not fae?"

He makes a deep, rumbling sound halfway between a laugh and a growl. "I am not fae. I am what humans call the devil." I want to look away; I *should* look away. All the words dry up in my throat, and I swallow. My trembling fingers find the scar on my chest, and I try to calm myself by taking a deep breath. Marius must notice my reaction, because he cocks his head and continues, "You are mine, Elizabeth Blackstone. My blood runs through your veins, and you are not safe unless you are with me. Eighteen years ago, your mother promised me your hand in marriage. Eighteen years ago, you took half of my power. Your mother tried to hide you," he says, his lips pressing together, "but you are mine. Now, forever, always."

My body trembles, and I try to back up a

step on my knees, but Marius reaches out for me, securing his large, warm fingers around my wrist.

"Follow me home, or I will force you," he growls.

I don't say anything. I'm afraid the burn of bile in my throat will turn into full-on vomiting if I don't get out of this bathroom. If I don't get away from *him*.

After a few seconds of us staring at each other, he stands and offers his hand to me. I stare at it and say the only thing I can think to say in a moment like this.

"Where are your other clothes?" My eyes sweep over his modern attire. "The red jacket?"

"These are less conspicuous in case anyone comes down here," he grumbles, his voice husky.

My hand is shaking as I place it in his, and he pulls me up to my feet with way too much ease.

I pull my hand out of his instantly. "Don't I have any say in all of this?"

His eyes darken, and he gives me a sullen look. "No."

Before I have a chance to respond, he pulls me into his chest, and we both fall backward through the mirror to whatever literal hellhole he crawled out of.

Four
LIZ

It's not a hellhole, though.

It's a motherfucking *castle*.

I look around as Marius walks away, leaving me alone in what appears to be a study. A fireplace taller than me stands in the center of the room, a large fire crackling. Ornate Persian rugs are layered on the floor, covering what looks like white marble. Lush, puffy couches sit in the middle of the room, and every wall except for the one with a fireplace has built-in shelves—and on the shelves are *thousands* of books. I turn and gawk at the doorway Marius exited through, spying room after room beyond it, with what looks like a staircase at the end.

I quickly walk after Marius, finding him standing at the base of the stairs, his eyebrows knitting together in annoyance.

"Rory sent these," he says, handing me my bag and coat.

I take them from him and follow him up the stairs.

"Do I get a tour of the place I will spend eternity in?"

Marius twirls around, his large body towering over me. "Eternity?"

"Yeah. Don't fae live forever?"

At that, one side of his lips lifts ever so slightly. "No. And you're only half fae." He turns around and continues to march up the stairs. "You'll probably live for two hundred years, at the most."

My mouth drops open. "Really?"

"If you don't get yourself killed before then."

I nod. "Fair enough."

He stops on the second floor, and we go right. The wood floors have dark red runners, and sconces line the wallpapered walls. It's gorgeous—the dark, floral wallpaper, the dark wood, the decorative rugs... It's a place born of another time.

"Your quarters are connected to mine," he says casually, and I stop walking. He turns to face me. "What?"

I look at the large, wooden double doors just behind him. "So you can just barge in whenever you want to?"

Marius' expression darkens. "I think you've forgotten the bargain your mother made. You are *mine*."

I lift my chin and take a step toward him in defiance. "That doesn't give you the right to act like a possessive animal," I snarl. "If you think I'm going to fuck you whenever you want to—"

Marius charges forward, shoving me against the wall. His eyes burn orange-red, and his nostrils flare. "If I wanted to fuck you, I would have already, Elizabeth."

I clench my jaw. "I want a lock on my door," I say calmly, trying to quell the fury roaring inside of me. "One that keeps you *out*."

Marius stares at me for a few heartbeats before letting me go. "Very well." He turns and pushes the doors open, and I try not to gasp at the opulence.

A formal sitting room with jewel-toned velvet lounge chairs, a large, gilded mirror on the mantle, and vases of fresh flowers await me. It's very feminine. I arch a brow as I take in the details of the room. I walk over to the window, trying not to act surprised when I see my city sprawled out below us, the twinkling lights flickering against the navy blue of the sky.

"Where are we?" I ask, crossing my arms.

"At the top of Allermuir Hill," he murmurs from behind me. "There's a glamour on the castle."

I nod once. "If you're the King of the Underworld, shouldn't you be, like, in hell?" I turn around, and he gives me a small, amused smile.

"Hell isn't a physical place. It exists in tandem with this life."

I swallow. "So, the fiery, cave-like place is all a myth?"

He crosses his arms and stands up taller. "I didn't say that. Those places exist, and I rule them from afar. But the home I choose to keep is here, in Scotland."

I study his tanned face, his large hands… the way he seems so weary and yet in a constant bad mood. I guess I would be, too, if I was the devil.

"What about your horns?" I ask, not sure I want to know the answer.

With a flourish of his hands, the horns reappear, as does a long, thick, barbed tail, and his fire-toned eyes. "Horns, a tail, demonic eyes…" His lips quirk upward. "Humans got a few things right about me, I suppose."

A tail.

I keep my eyes on him as he turns around, horns and tail gone. As I follow him deeper into the shared quarters, everything starts to sink in. I slow my pace as my heart begins to pound, both from the crazy and strange turn of events, but also… how long will it take for people to realize that I'm gone? My chest caves when I think about how one second, I was getting a drink in Edinburgh, and the next, I am in this castle, crashing with the fucking devil. It's like someone flipped a switch, and then I was gone. Aside from Rory… would anyone check up on me? Would people file a missing person's report? My eyes prick at the thought, and I mindlessly follow Marius to a set of twin doors.

He gestures to the one on the right. "Your room."

I stare at the door for a second before looking at him, the fury from a minute ago beginning to bubble up again.

"So, I'm just supposed to live here with you until I die? Am I understanding correctly?"

Marius's eyes flash with irritation as he purses his lips. "You are to be my wife, and everything that entails."

"Wonderful," I snap out.

"You will find everything you need in your suite. Dinner is at eight." He twists and enters his room before slamming it closed behind him.

"Everything except freedom," I mutter, opening the door and looking around the luxurious suite.

After closing the door, I take in the large bedroom. There's a four-poster bed with matching, light blue side tables. All the furniture—a dresser, wardrobe, and desk—are of the same rich, dark wood. A navy-blue couch sits beneath the massive window, and rugs are layered on the floor to keep it feeling cozy. Whether or not he did it on purpose, I'm not sure–but the fire is going, giving the room an odd sense of warmth and comfort. I walk to the bathroom, and it's just as ornate. Marble floors and walls, brass fixtures, and a large, claw-foot tub that overlooks what appears to be a meadow. Scoffing, I walk back to the bedroom and grab my purse.

There's no way he decorated this place himself. It's too stylish, too thoughtful for a brute like him. I switch my phone back on, and to my surprise, it works. I have two text messages from Shepherd, and when I open them up, my throat constricts. I sit down on the bed to read them.

Shepherd: Liz, can we talk?

Shepherd: Please, baby. I need to talk to you. Call me back ASAP.

Just to make sure Marius didn't mess with my cell phone, I humor Shepherd and shoot a text back.

Me: I have nothing to say to you.

It says it's delivered, and relief washes over me when it changes to *Read*. At least my phone still works; at least I'm still connected to my regular life. I haven't even finished setting it down on the bed beside me when there's a knock on the door. I stiffen, staying silent. If Marius is a demon, what other kinds of creatures live here? Rory and I are apparently fae. And if fae and demons exist, what else exists just underneath the surface of a glamour? How many creatures have I seen in my day-to-day life, and how many does Marius keep in his household? I'm just about to call out when there's another knock.

"Ms. Blackstone? May I enter?"

I didn't expect a female's voice, and that fact makes me feel a tiny bit better.

"Come in," I answer.

A woman enters, and the only distinguishing paranormal thing about her is her delicately pointed ears. Other than that, she looks like a regular human—short, black hair; a petite, lithe body; and warm, brown eyes. She smiles and walks over to me, a tablet in her hand.

"So nice to finally meet you, Elizabeth," she purrs, her voice like velvet. She has an American accent, and she's smiling way too much for someone who works for the devil, in my opinion. "I'm Annabelle. I am one of Marius's employees."

"He has employees?"

She nods, her delicate features softening as she smiles even wider. "Hundreds, actually," she answers, tapping something into the tablet. "I'm here to help you acclimate to your new living quarters. I just wanted to ask you a few questions, if that's okay?"

I nod. "Sure. I get the feeling I don't really have a choice, do I?"

She gives me a conspiratorial smile. "I'm afraid not. But, if it helps, Marius is a kind man. I've loved my time working for him, and my partner and I live in the east wing if you ever need anything."

I take in what she's telling me, my eyes roving over her casual jeans and tank top attire. "Are you fae?"

She shakes her head. "Just a regular faerie. My partner is half-vampire." I open and close my mouth. I was right—there are all sorts of creatures living here. Annabelle must see my hesitation, because she tilts her head. "She's a vegetarian," she explains, laughing. "And because she's only half vampire, she eats regular food, too."

I don't want to contemplate the fact that I'm living with a vampire too long.

Not like the devil is any safer, though.

"What's the difference between faeries and fae?"

She smiles. "There are three classes of what humans call faeries. I am a classic faerie—small, pointed ears, and I can fly around if needed," she explains. "Then there's the fae, who look like humans—except they have incredible power. You are fae. Last, there's the high fae—the rulers of our kind. They usually don't associate with us, and they stick to their colonies with other high fae, presiding over faerie politics."

I nod. "So, faeries, vampires, and demons?"

She cocks her head. "And trolls, goblins, angels, centaurs, dragons, jinn, mermaids, monsters—"

"I get it," I interrupt, feeling my stomach roll with nausea again.

"I can explain more another time," she says, her voice friendly. "I just need to ask a few questions, and then I can let you change for dinner. There are some clothes in the dresser, by the way," she adds.

"Okay."

She taps her tablet again. "Right. I just need your size, height, and clothing preference."

I open and close my mouth. "I have clothes," I explain, thinking of my tiny flat on the outskirts of Edinburgh.

She smirks. "I can send for those if you'd like, but Marius wants you to feel comfortable here. It might be nice to have a fresh start."

"I'd like my old clothes," I reply, my voice obstinate. "But if he insists on buying me new ones, I'm not picky. I'm a size 12."

She nods once, inputting something on the tablet. "Height?"

I shrug. "About five foot seven."

"Lovely. And what about personal items? Do you have any preferences? Things like toothpaste, shampoo, foundation..." She trails off, her eyes grazing over my unkempt hair and makeup-less face.

"I don't care. If he's going to keep me here as his prisoner, does it really matter what kind of shampoo I use?"

Annabelle purses her lips and shifts her weight from one hip to the other. She moves like a ballerina, graceful and sure-footed.

"You are not a prisoner," Annabelle says gently. "You are to be Marius's wife—"

"I understand that," I grit out, my fists clenching at my side. "But what people are failing to see is that I have no say in the matter. I just wanted to get a drink, and the next thing I knew, I was told I was betrothed to some man who claims to be the devil, living in a castle hidden from humans, getting asked what kind of *shampoo* I use?" My voice rises with every sentence. "This whole thing is just the cherry on top of the shittiest week of my life. Quite frankly, I don't care about clothing, or shampoo. All I want is to leave and go back to my flat," I finish, my voice breaking.

Annabelle sits down on the bed next to

me; her presence feeling oddly comforting. "I understand all of that, Elizabeth."

"Liz," I say quickly, swiping my wet cheek. "Everyone calls me Liz."

"Okay, Liz. I understand how you must be feeling. It's quite a shock. Going from your human life to this new life... you probably have a whiplash." She scoots a tiny bit closer. "I don't know the exact circumstances, only what the valet told me a few moments ago. But maybe I can explain it woman to woman, if that would help?" I shrug, and she continues, "Your mother made a blood bond with Marius eighteen years ago. Those can't be broken. They are bargains made with blood, and if you or Marius break or defy a blood bond, both parties will perish."

I suck in a sharp breath, but Annabelle reaches out for my hand, sending out the same sort of comforting feeling Marius sent through me earlier, when he came through the mirror.

"On top of that, your mother was a full fae, and had substantial powers. She was able to glamour you, hide your scent, and place you in a bubble, essentially. For some reason, when you uttered Marius's name, it shattered that glamour, hence why Marius was able to find you." More tears prick at my eyes, and Annabelle keeps talking. "He's been searching for you for as long as I can remember."

"If my mother was fae, how could she possibly have died from Alzheimer's?" I ask. It's the question that's been burning through my mind all evening.

Annabelle shrugs. "Mythical creatures are susceptible to human ailments."

I sniff. "So, you're saying I have to stay, because if I leave, if I defy Marius and refuse to become his bride, we'll both die?"

She nods. "Yes. Even if you could somehow go back to your old life, the glamour is gone now. Plus, Marius's demon blood runs through your veins. You're a hybrid, and a strong one at that. And other supernatural creatures will sense that. It's very easy to take advantage of an unsuspecting fae, and a lot of people want to harm Marius. They would have no problem harming you and harnessing his power through you. That's why you're safest here, with him."

I digest all the information she's telling me. My mother establishing a blood bond with

Marius, being fae, being *here*, talking to a real-life Tinkerbell…

"I think I just need a few minutes to take this all in," I say slowly.

Annabelle stands. "Of course. I'll see you at dinner, Liz."

She leaves the room before I can respond.

I lie down on the bed, and everything that happened today makes my chest constricted. Shepherd and Rachel, Dante's Inferno and everything that happened there, how my life is now that of some strange, kept wife, fae-demon hybrid. My chest cracks open, and I start sobbing. Losing my job is enough of a tear-jerker. But losing my best friend, boyfriend, and entire life in one day? It feels like it's too much. I curl up, clutching the soft duvet to my chest as I let it all out. I have to find a way out of this bargain—a way to break the blood bond that keeps both Marius and me safe. There *has* to be a way.

I vow to spend tomorrow figuring out how I can get out of this situation.

My eyelids get heavy, and I don't even attempt to keep myself awake to attend dinner.

As I drift off, I can't help but think, even if I could go back to my regular life, what's waiting for me?

What is left for me to go back to?

Nothing, I tell myself.

The heavy ache in my chest deepens, and I finally let myself succumb to sleep.

Five
MARY

Eighteen Years Ago

My fingers get caught in my tangled hair as I attempt to run them through my long, red hair. Trembling, I shake my hand out and manage to pull my hair up into a ponytail as I pace the waiting room. It feels as though someone has taken an eggbeater and is scrambling my insides. It's pure torture, and every sound, every click of a faraway door, sends me scanning the room and listening for the footsteps of Elizabeth's doctor. I'm not sure if my heightened hearing, smell, and vision is helping the situation, or if it's just making me more anxious.

Elizabeth.

My baby.

A faraway door opens, and I direct my fae ears to listen to the cadence of the footsteps.

It's him.

I'm running out of the waiting room before anyone can say anything, my speed just a tad too quick to be fully human. But I don't care. I don't give a shit who sees me. That doctor was operating on my toddler—my two-year-old, the love and joy of my life. I *have* to know that she's okay. Of course, they keep all operating rooms behind large, silver doors so that supernatural ears can't listen in on any surgery. I only know that because I spent most of my morning trying to break down the metal barrier with no success.

Doctor Godfry is covered in blood, and I whimper at the sight. His weathered face is weary, and he doesn't see me at first—doesn't expect the crazy, loco mother to assault him right outside of the operating room.

"Doctor," I say, my voice low.

His eyes snap to mine, surprise shadowing his features. He looks around, probably wondering how I got here so quickly.

"I was using the restroom," I lie.

He nods, a sad smile on his face. "Mrs. Blackstone, why don't you take a seat?"

I know what that means, and my heart pounds inside of me as I sit on the nearest chair. The doctor sits next to me, and I ignore the whooshing in my ears.

"We did everything we could, Mary," he explains, using my first name. He's been Elizabeth's cardiologist since before she was born; since I received the news of her heart condition still in my womb. "She's just too weak, too sick. Her heart muscles aren't bouncing back like I hoped. She's stable, and we could probably get her on the transplant waiting list, but with how quickly she's been deteriorating…" He reaches out for my hand. "I hesitate to say this, but I think you should prepare to say goodbye. We did everything we could."

A sob leaves my throat, my vision tilting.

"She's just a baby," I whisper. "She just had her second birthday party," I say, hoping it will make all of this go away.

Doctor Godfry squeezes my hand.

"Unfortunately, we always knew this might be a possibility," he says softly. "She had two pain-free years. Now, all we can do is give her a peaceful goodbye."

I shake my head. "No." Suddenly, I know what I must do. Standing, I take a deep breath. "I'll be right back," I say, walking away.

I walk out of the hallway, out of the waiting room, and out of the hospital. My feet are confident, steady on the cobblestone as I walk down the street, entering Dante's Inferno. I don't come here much. We all know what awaits us in the bathroom. Right now, however, I don't care. Right now, I need a miracle.

And a miracle is what I'm about to beg for.

Don't do it, my mind screams at me. But I don't listen, because right now, I'll sacrifice anything to save my daughter. *Do* anything.

I take the winding steps down into the bowels of Edinburgh, down to where the portal exists, unbeknownst to humans. I barge into the bathroom and lean against the vanity, taking a deep breath. Growing up, we were all warned never to make deals with Bloody Marius. The legend of Marius was one that gave me nightmares, and I wasn't sure he was real until last year.

Until Lars left me, and I wound up down here with some friends, and a man appeared in the mirror. We all ran away screaming, and I vowed to myself I'd never come back here. But then Elizabeth got worse, and three surgeries later, she was going to die if I didn't do something.

Marius.

My skin crawls with goosebumps as I take a deep breath.

"Save her, please," I whisper. "Bloody Marius," I add, summoning him. His name—that's all it took. When I look up, I see a man is watching me on the other side of the mirror. He's wearing a linen shirt, and his dark hair is mussed up, as if I stirred him from sleep. "She's going to die if I don't save her," I tell him, my voice breaking.

What am I doing?

He pushes through the glass, and I step back as he appears before me. "What is your sacrifice?"

Another sob escapes my throat. "Anything.

You can have anything."

He nods. "Take me to her."

I don't say anything as he follows me out of the bathroom, out of the bar, and into the streets of Edinburgh. When I look behind me, I can see that he's changed into jeans and a t-shirt. I swallow as we weave through the waiting room, down the hallway, and when I ask the desk where my daughter is recovering from surgery, they tell me.

Marius follows.

There is a nurse in the room, and she jumps up once she sees me. I recognize her from earlier.

"Mrs. Blackstone," she says quickly. "Elizabeth is still sleeping," she adds, looking down at my daughter.

I follow her gaze, and my throat dries up. My daughter—my light—looks so small, so frail. She's in a diaper, covered partially by a generic woven blanket. Her chest is covered in bandages, and I can't help but notice how her breathing is labored.

"Dr. Godfry will be in soon," she says, looking behind me at Marius.

"My brother," I say quickly, and she just

nods once. "She will be awake soon."

She leaves Marius, Elizabeth, and me alone in the hospital room.

"Help her," I beg him.

He looks between us, his brows furrowed. I see him clench his fists once, and then he walks over to my daughter. Looking down at her, something I can't discern passes over his face, and he reaches down for her tiny arm.

"You wish for me to heal her completely?" he asks, looking back up at me.

I nod vigorously. "Yes. Do whatever you have to."

"And what will you give me in return?" he asks again. His gold eyes pin me to the spot. Elizabeth stirs, and he looks down at her as she opens her eyes. "Her," he whispers.

I'm sure I don't hear him correctly at first. "Pardon?"

Marius looks back up at me. "When she is of age, she will become my wife."

My blood cools. "No," I whisper.

He drops her arm, taking a step back. "Very well." Turning to go, he's almost to the door when I concede.

"Why?" I ask, my voice small in the large room.

He twists around to face me again. "Because to heal her, I will need to give her my blood. If you agree that she can be mine when she's old enough to marry, then I will save her. But only if I can guarantee we will be reunited."

My mind is spinning.

All I hear is *I will save her.*

"Fine," I whisper. I will figure out how to protect her from him later. Once she's healthy—once I don't have her inevitable death hanging over me.

Marius steps forward and raises his arm, placing the inside part against his mouth. When he pulls it away, I see a bloody bite mark. He bends down and places his wrist in Elizabeth's mouth. She latches immediately, and her eyes widen as she sucks. After a few seconds, he tries to pull his wrist away, but both of Elizabeth's hands come up and hold him in place. She's gulping quickly now, and I see her cheeks flush with color, her eyes go from sunken and nearly black to their normal, large, honey-colored state.

"Elizabeth," I warn. "Let him go."

Her eyes find me, and she shakes her head once. Marius's face is pale; his eyes bright red.

"Elizabeth," he growls, and at that, she unlatches. He steadies himself on the railing of the hospital bed, his chest heaving quickly. He turns to me. "It is done. She took more than enough to heal what ails her." He casts one more look down at my daughter before turning his gaze back to me. "I expect you to keep your end of the bargain, Mary Blackstone."

Over my dead body.

Before I can protest, he vanishes.

When I look over at my daughter, she is smiling at me—full of life, full of energy.

For her future, I don't regret what I did.

I would've done anything to save her.

And now, I will do everything in my power to keep that monster away from her.

Six
MARIUS

Present

I CLENCH AND UNCLENCH MY FISTS AT MY SIDE AS I pace my room, the warmth from the fire causing my skin to tingle. I walk over to my desk and take another sip of espresso.

She is in shock.

She is young and naive.

She was taken from her entire life and placed in a strange place.

There are a multitude of reasons why Elizabeth did not show up for dinner last night. I did not order her, because when I glanced into her room last night, she was fast asleep on the bed. Her heavy breathing was slow and contented, but her face was pinched, her expression fretful. I almost ran a finger down her smooth skin, but I was afraid of disturbing her, especially after she expressed worry about me barging in whenever I wanted to. She reminded me so much of her young self, sleeping like that.

So, I left her to sleep, but made sure Annabelle left some food for her in case she woke up hungry. Now it's half past six, and I continue to pace my bedroom, using my heightened sense of hearing to listen for any noise coming from her room.

There's a knock at my door, and I raise a hand to open it from across the room. Annabelle stands on the other side, and she nods once before she pushes through. I hide my smile at how she's the most organized person in this household.

And the earliest to rise.

"Morning," she chirps. I grumble something unintelligible in response. "I was just wondering if you'd still planned to visit Adeñata this morning?"

I rub my lower lip with my hand, sighing.

"Yeah. I haven't been back in two months. I should check up on Ciro, keep him on his toes."

She taps something into her tablet. "Wonderful. Your car is booked, and everything is all set. Will you be staying at your place, or should I book you into one of the hotels?"

"My place," I reply, and her eyebrows raise a fraction of an inch. She doesn't say anything as she taps the screen again.

"Okay. Shall I have travel clothes added to Elizabeth's wardrobe, then?"

"Yes." I thumb my nose. "Is she awake?" I ask casually.

Annabelle smirks. "Not yet. Would you like me to wake her?"

I look away. "No. Let her sleep."

"All right, your plane will be ready at nine. Breakfast in thirty minutes."

I nod. "Thank you, Annabelle."

She just gives me a smile before walking out of the bedroom, her sneakers hardly making a sound due to her light feet. I swear, a heavy breeze could blow her away. Once she's gone, I continue pacing, eventually getting dressed. Throwing on my human clothes, I tie my boots and comb through my hair before standing against the wall I share with Elizabeth. I can hear her beginning to stir, the scent of fear potent and wafting into my room. I roll my sleeves up a bit and exit my bedroom, stalking to her door and knocking three times.

Her small voice makes my chest ache. "Come in," she says, and I throw the door open.

She's still in bed, the duvet rumpled around her. She must've taken her clothes off at some point, because they sit in a pile next to the bed. I swallow at the thought of her being nearly naked under the covers.

"Breakfast is at seven," I tell her. "We depart for Adeñata at nine, and you will accompany me."

Her body stiffens, and she glares at me. "What's Adeñata?"

I cross my arms. "An underground prison. Those fiery hellscapes you mentioned yesterday? It's like that."

Her eyes widen. "Really?"

I nod. "The really bad people are sent there after they die. There's no fire, but the damp, underground prison isn't necessarily a vacation, either."

"Why am I going with you?"

I huff a laugh. "Because the man who runs the prison is an arrogant piece of shit. I want to flaunt you; I want him to see the power you hold within yourself. I want him to quake in his boots, because he needs to be taken down a peg."

She shifts, her hands pulling the covers tighter around her chest. I notice the pink edge of her scar peeking out.

"I don't think I have power," she says, sounding irritated.

"You have been glamoured your entire life, Elizabeth. Just like when you charred Rory's shirt, it will come in waves right now—until something unleashes it."

Her honey-colored eyes widen further. "Will it hurt?"

I smile. "No. It won't hurt. But it may surprise you, and it may hurt someone else if we're not careful." She opens her mouth to retort, but I hold a hand up. "I'll see you at breakfast."

"What if I don't want to go?" she says as I

reach the door.

I turn to face her. "You don't have a choice."

She frowns. "Of course I don't."

I press my lips together and crack my neck. Her defiance is a fucking pain in my arse. "I have provided you with everything you could ever need. I promise you, if your mother had made a blood bargain with some other monster, they would not be fretting over what to serve you for breakfast."

"My mother never intended for me to marry you," she spits, baring her teeth. "She would've let me *die* before subjecting me to this nightmare." Her voice is cruel, biting. And her eyes… they're glowing orange. "There must be way out of this bargain, and I'm going to find it."

"You have my blood," I grit out.

"So take it back!" she shouts, her cheeks reddening.

"If I take my blood back, you will die," I growl, raising my voice to match hers. "Beside that point, blood bonds cannot be broken. If they are, both parties—"

"Yeah, yeah," she mumbles, rolling her

eyes. "Both parties die. So what? I'd rather be dead than be married to you."

Her words make me grit my teeth, as I try to ignore the heaviness in my chest and the tightness in my throat.

Fuck this.

I turn to leave, slamming the door closed behind me, ignoring the smell of smoke emanating from Elizabeth's room.

She can burn for all I care.

Seven
LIZ

"What the hell is that?" I ask incredulously. "I'm not wearing that."

Annabelle holds up what looks to be a minidress, the slit going so high that I'm pretty sure I'd need to wax every inch of skin from the waist down.

Annabelle's eyes twinkle with mirth. "Adeñata is unlike any city, Liz. They have... ideas about how women should act."

I roll my eyes. "Apparently Marius shares those ideas—"

"Actually," she says, smiling, "He's very progressive for someone of his time. I am his first commander—a faerie, who are considered lesser beings, and a lesbian at that."

I twist my lips to the side. "Yeah, but he has me wearing *that*," I whine.

She sighs, sitting down on the chair next to the bed. "Marius rules the underworld," she murmurs. "It is not a good place for women—and certainly not powerful fae women with demon blood," she adds, winking. "By dressing the part, it signals that you are with him. Not as his employee, but as his intended *wife*." I resist the urge to roll my eyes. Annabelle continues, "Trust me, that has way more sway with these creatures. Marius does not expect you to dress a certain way here. He does not hold those views here, in his home. But in Adeñata? You are safer if people can visually see that you are *with* Marius," she explains.

I don't like it, but I understand the reasoning.

"Fine," I concede. "I'll wear a dress to signify that I'm going to be his *wife*," I bite out, "but I'm not wearing that flimsy piece of fabric."

Annabelle hops up, looking pleased. "We can find you something," she says coyly, walking over to the wardrobe and throwing it open. My mouth drops open. Beyond the confines of the wardrobe, an entire *room* sits behind it—like an enchanted closet. And the racks are full of what I can tell are designer clothes. Silks and velvet and fur… there's even a shoe rack in the back, lit up to highlight the different pairs of sneakers Marius obviously had someone pick out for me. "Go ahead," she says, gesturing to the expanse of clothing. "Take your pick."

Annabelle gives me a quick tour around the castle. I stop counting after the ninth bedroom, and then we meander downstairs, touring the kitchen, living room, and dining room. Breakfast will be served any minute, but Annabelle shows me the garden through a set of double doors. For the umpteenth time, my jaw drops as I take in the meadow and forest beyond the gothic-style rose garden. Stone arches and black roses make up a lot of the garden, and when we walk back into the house, I realize just how much it pains me to admit that I love the style of the house.

Old, eerie, yet beautiful in a moody sort of

way, it's everything I love about Scotland and old castles. There's always a fire going, and the furniture is fancy yet lived in—the couches all sag in the middle, the fabric slightly worn. The wallpaper is spectacular, curated for each room to give off a different vibe. The dark furniture is outdated, but it fits within the castle, like it was chosen hundreds of years ago, and never updated. I hate that I love it.

I follow Annabelle into the formal dining room, and Marius is already seated at the table. He's in the same red jacket as before, the gilded stitching reflecting the light from the chandelier above us. He has on black pants and black dress shoes. His eyes sweep over my dress—a knee-length, dark red, silk number that's form-fitting while also not too revealing like the washcloth he picked out. *Pig*. I had Annabelle sweep my hair to the side and braid it loosely, and I slipped into heeled sandals because I was told the weather would be warm. I swear, I see his pupils glow orange for a second before they rove back up to my eyes.

"You didn't like the dress I picked out for you?" he asks, rubbing his mouth with his hand. The anger and fury in his expression from earlier is still there.

"I'm here to accompany you as your future wife. Not your fucking concubine."

Marius slams his hand on the table, startling me. "You are here because your mother made a bargain with me. And you've been here for less than a day. You have no idea—"

"Marius," Annabelle warns, shaking her head.

His nostrils flare but he sits up straighter and places his palms face down on the table. "Very well. Sit and eat," he commands, sweeping his hand over the plethora of food available to us.

I look between him and Annabelle. *Interesting.* She seems to have way more influence over him than I gave her credit for. Maybe she can help me find a way out of this stupid bargain.

I sit down, and my eyes scan the food as my stomach audibly growls. I didn't eat dinner last night, and my mouth waters as I grab a buttery croissant, some sausage, and freshly scrambled eggs. Annabelle leaves once she can guarantee we won't rip each other's heads off, leaving

Marius and I alone to eat in silence. I don't complain, though, because I was hungrier than I thought. I devour my first serving, and for my second serving, I help myself to plain yogurt and fruit, refilling my coffee cup as well. Marius just sips his coffee and watches me, but it feels too good to eat to care.

Finally, I lean back and groan, my hand resting on my stomach. "That was delicious," I say, turning to face him.

He doesn't smile. Instead, he pushes out from the table and grabs a banana. "I'll see you by the front door at a quarter to nine." And then he turns to go, stalking away.

"Goodbye to you too, asshole," I mutter, finishing my coffee.

I walk back up the stairs to my room, making sure I don't have food in my teeth before grabbing my phone and a shawl. I slip the shawl around my shoulders and head downstairs with five minutes to spare.

Marius is already waiting by the door, and he gives me an irritated look before throwing the front door open for me. He gestures for me to walk ahead. Holding my chin—and dignity—

high, I climb into the black car awaiting us just outside. I climb to the other side, and Marius joins me, closing the door and silencing us inside the luxury vehicle.

"Why the Beauty and the Beast clothes?" I ask, giving his outfit the side-eye.

I can't say I mind, though—not really. His black hair and scruff look good in the antique clothes. Like the castle, he's suited to another time, and seeing him in modern clothes is almost strange. He's too angled, too brooding, to sport cheap cotton. No, his large physique—complete with bulging biceps, large hands, tapered waist, and muscular legs—really needed the clothes to show off just how brutal and primordial he was.

"Because I like them," he answers, looking out of the window as we drive away from the castle.

"Can't you teleport us to Adera—"

"Adeñata," he corrects.

My nostrils flare. "*Adeñata*," I repeat, not caring about how my voice sounds sassy and bratty. "You teleported us from the bar. Why are we driving to the airport?"

Marius sighs. "Do you always ask this many

questions?"

"I don't have a valid passport," I answer, because I can't think of anything else to explain my unease at this entire situation.

At this, I swear his lips twitch with a hint of a smile. "You won't need a passport. We are taking my private jet."

"But why can't you teleport—"

"That's enough questions, Elizabeth," he growls, looking at me with red eyes.

I know I should drop my eyes, but I don't. Instead, I hold his stare for what feels like minutes. Finally, he sighs again.

"I prefer to fly," he says simply.

I scowl. "But—"

In a flash, he moves his body so that he's pinning me against the window. One of his hands comes around my throat, and he presses harder so hard that I can barely breath. My eyes bulge, and he bares his teeth as he lets out a low growl from deep within his chest. He must be using his blood power, because I can't move. My arms remain at my side.

"If I wanted to, I could transport us to any place, of any time period. The rules of time don't apply to me." I gasp for air, and he loosens his grip ever so slightly. "If I wanted to, I could turn this car to ash—I could level this city to cinders. This country. This *earth*. I'm not *teleporting* us." He sneers, his lips an inch from my face. "Because I like to fly the plane myself. Because this life can be fucking boring, and sometimes, I don't want to take the easy way out."

He releases me, and I fall forward as my hands come up to my neck. I cough a couple of times, and Marius goes back to scowling out of his window.

"You could've just said you wanted to fly," I mutter, glaring at the back of his stupid head.

The rest of the ten-minute drive is uneventful, and the driver drops us off at a lone airplane hangar in the middle of a field. I get the feeling that this hangar is hidden from human eyes by a glamour. I hop out of the car and stare at the plane before us. Biting my tongue, I follow Marius into the modern private jet. He's taken his jacket off, as the day is starting to warm up, and his black dress shirt is rolled up to his elbows. The door opens, and he gestures for me to climb up the stairs first. I'm still fuming from what he did in the car, so I find a seat in the very back and plan to ignore him for the entirety of the flight.

A few minutes later, I can hear him talking into the headset he has on, and I try not to pay attention to the way his corded arms grip the throttle. I sink into the buttery leather seat, propping my feet up on the leather footstool. Buckling myself, I cross my arms and look out the window as the engine purrs to life.

I'm being flown around Europe by the devil. No big deal.

We take off a few minutes later, and shortly after, we're high enough that Marius must have the plane on autopilot. He stands up and wanders to the passenger area, kneeling next to a refrigerator and grabbing a water.

His eyes find mine as he drinks, and he offers me a new bottle.

"Drink," he instructs. "It's very warm where we're going."

"Should feel like home to you, then," I retort.

He cocks his head. "I didn't want this either, Elizabeth. But your mother was so desperate to save you. If you're going to blame anyone, blame her for offering your life and maidenhood to me."

I burst out laughing. "My maidenhood? That ship sailed a looooong time ago."

He flattens his lips, and his eyes burn red. "Is that so?"

I sit up straighter. "Perhaps that's a dealbreaker for you?"

Maybe it's a way out of the bargain. Who knows… he lives like he's still in the 1600s. Maybe there's a chance he won't want me if he knows I'm not a virgin. Men used to kill women for less.

But he just chuckles, rolling his tongue around on the inside of his cheek. "Definitely not a dealbreaker. Except, humans are so… gentle. I don't know if that counts."

My stomach flips. "Is that so?" I say sarcastically.

He gives me a crooked smile. "The first time you fuck someone who isn't human, you'll realize you've never truly been fucked before, Elizabeth."

He turns and walks back to the cockpit. The

rebuttal I had planned gets stuck in my throat. I grind my jaw and take a deep breath, reaching up and turning up the fan so that it will cool my hot skin. Hearing Marius saying the word *fucked* makes me feel all funny inside, and I refuse to catch feelings for a man who essentially kidnapped me against my will.

I need to find a way out of this bargain.

I scroll through my social media as we fly. Thankfully, the plane is equipped with Wi-Fi. I block Shepherd after several missed calls and swallow the bile in my throat when I think about the fact that my best friend can't even find the courage to text me and apologize for what she did. Rachel was my ride or die, my soulmate, and the whole cheating thing hurts more when I think of how she betrayed me.

She'd get a kick out of all of this, that's for sure.

I swipe at my eyes and look down at the floor, putting my phone away and kicking my sandals off. Pulling my knees to my chest, I watch the clouds go by as we fly for who knows how long.

About two hours later, I feel the plane begin

to descend, and I sit up and slip my shoes back on to get ready for landing. Marius manages a smooth landing, and then we pull into a tiny airport on a cliff, overlooking what appears to be the Mediterranean Sea. Beyond the small airport, terracotta buildings line the coast, and the sand is a glittering mass of black and silver swirls. It's stunning. The plane turns off, and the door opens automatically. I grab my things and walk out, only to be greeted by yet another black car. It's hot, but I'm only outside for a second before climbing into the air-conditioned car.

Marius comes up behind me and directs me into the back seat, and we drive away from the airport.

"Where are we?" I ask, my eyes taking in the unfamiliar location.

"Humans consider this Northern Spain," he answers, his voice sounding bored. "But when they lay eyes upon this area, it looks like a dilapidated fishing port."

"You all love to glamour things, don't you?"

His eyes narrow. "You all? Did you forget that you're a powerful fae with demon blood, or are you still in denial?"

I shrug. "I don't know how to glamour things."

"Well, maybe we should change that."

Before I can ask what he means, we pull up to what can only be described as an arena. Stone pillars enclose a large dirt ring, and several people are lined up, hands clasped in front of them as if they're waiting for us.

"You have one job while we're here, Elizabeth," Marius murmurs as he leans in close. "Act like you want to be standing next to me," he purrs. "I'm putting a glamour on you so that they can't sniff out my blood," he adds, grabbing my hand. "Understood?"

I nod. What other choice do I have?

Eight
LIZ

MARIUS OPENS THE DOOR FOR ME, AND I TAKE his hand as he helps me out onto the dirt. He wasn't joking when he said it would be hot here, and in the arena, there's zero shade. The sun beats down on me, and I already know I should've had more water. My dress immediately begins to stick to my skin. Marius takes my hand, and we walk to where the other people are gathered. Shielding my eyes with my free hand, I scan their faces for any paranormal features, but they look like humans. Perhaps they are. They're all wearing beige colors, and they're mostly in drapey, loose warm weather clothing that speaks of a different culture.

We stop a few feet away, and to my surprise, all five of the people here drop down to their knees before Marius. My eyebrows shoot up as I look over at him, but he has a mask of indifference plastered on his beautiful face.

"Luciano, Sofia, Isabel, Augustine, Ciro," he says, by way of greeting. "I'd like to introduce you to my fiancée," he adds.

All five of them dip their heads further, and none of them look up at me. Their dedication impresses me, especially since the women are wearing skirts, and their knees must be screaming in pain from kneeling in the grit.

"You may rise," he instructs, and all five of them stand without so much as a brushing off their now-dirty knees. They all watch Marius. "I assume all is well in Adeñata."

The man on the left nods once. "It is, my king."

King?

"And the issue you were all having last month... it has been taken care of?"

One of the other men answers, "Yes, Your Majesty. It has been taken care of." It's then that

I realize none of the women have looked up—none of them have so much as moved, their bodies still and unmoving.

The third man looks up at Marius, and then he pins his gaze on me. My blood cools when our eyes meet, because his eyes don't have pupils.

They're just pure black.

I falter a bit, and Marius tugs me up discreetly so that I don't look like I'm about to faint from the heat.

"Your fiancée," he says, his voice sounding... harmonious. Like three different voices are coming out at once. "Last time we saw you, there was no mention of a fiancée. How did you two meet?"

My eyes go to the women, who are still looking at the ground.

Adeñata is unlike any city, Liz. They have... ideas about how women should act.

Fuck that.

"I got drunk, and we banged in the bathroom of a bar," I say cheerily. Both women's lips turn up ever so slightly, but the third man glares at me as I give him a simpering smile. Marius coughs and squeezes my hand so tightly that I nearly cry out.

"She's not wrong, Ciro. We met at a bar. I proposed shortly after."

The third man—Ciro—looks between us skeptically. "You would lower yourself so much as to marry a lowly fae?" he asks, the hatred in his voice evident by the way he stares at me with those creepy-as-fuck eyes.

"If you have a problem with my soon-to-be wife, there are ways to take care of that," Marius answers smoothly. "And if you disrespect her again, I will take care of it."

Ciro's face blanches. "Of course, my lord."

"Let's go, then. My fiancée is excited to see Adeñata with her own eyes."

I give all five of them a confident smile, and Marius tugs us forward to one of the iron doors that border the dirt ring. He doesn't look back to see if they're following, as he shoves the door open, revealing a large, stone cavern. It's massive, and we enter onto a balcony overlooking the immense, subterranean cave. It's eerily quiet, and the smell of smoke hits my nostrils. Instantly, my whole body goes rigid, and the sensation of fear, anguish, and suffering filter through my heightened senses. I drop Marius's hand, but he reaches out for it again and tugs me into his side.

"Are you brave enough to face this? Or do I need to glamour you?"

I swallow as someone screams. "I can do it," I answer, standing straighter.

He pulls us to the right, and we descend a large staircase down and down and down, winding past floors and floors of... prison cells.

Looking behind us, I can see that the five people from up above are a good deal behind us, so I lean in.

"What is this place?"

Marius's eyes flash red for a split second, and just then, another wail carries through the stone den.

"This is hell, Elizabeth." I glance around at all the cells, trying to do the math, but Marius continues whispering into my ear. I try not to shiver at the feel of his breath trailing the sensitive spot behind my ear. "Hell doesn't exist for normal humans," he murmurs. "The truly despicable humans are sent to purgatory, where they relive their worst nightmares, over and over again." I shiver, and I swear I can feel his lips tug into a smile against my skin at my reaction. "Monsters and immortal creatures, however, need someplace to go—someplace to live out eternity where they can be contained."

My jaw goes slack as another shriek echoes through the tunnels. *Not human*, I think. What kinds of beasts are imprisoned here?

"As a matter of fact, overruling the human realms and figuring out purgatory is seamless. Humans are easy, after all," he purrs. "But demons? Vampires? The high fae? They're not too easy, and sometimes, they escape. We have prisons on every continent, endless cells ready and waiting for anything supernatural."

I don't say anything as we emerge on the ground floor. "So why are we here today, then?" I ask, looking around at all the people buzzing around, all of them bowing when they notice Marius.

"To remind them who rules this place," Marius says, his voice low and deep. "The five people who met with us earlier? There used to be six." My skin pebbles. "To make sure everything is running as it should," he adds. "And to show you off, because it gets all of the witches off my back."

I huff a laugh, covering it with a cough. "Witches?"

He stops and gives me a wan smile, placing his hands in his pockets. Down here, in the dim light, he looks otherworldly.

"They're obsessed with me," he says, smirking. "A lot of them worship the devil, and that means trying to get me into bed every chance they get."

My lips twitch. "Do you ever take them up on it?"

His eyes gleam with something feral. "Of course. But they don't interest me," he says slowly.

"Why not?" I ask, my throat going dry as his eyes sweep over my face.

"Because I like the chase, the thrill of fucking someone who least expects it." I feel my face pale, and he grabs my arm, pulling me against his hard body. "I like excitement, and a little bit of fear. I like the *scent* of them not knowing what I'll do next. Witches know what to expect—they're gossips, and they speak among themselves. But someone who doesn't know me? Who doesn't know the amount of pleasure I'm capable of giving?" he purrs, and my knees go weak. He must sense the way my body reacts to him, because the hand on my back trails lower, grazing my ass. My skin is on fire, and my stomach clenches when he squeezes my ass cheek. "I like taking control, Elizabeth."

"Marius," a woman croons from behind him. I pull away from him and he lets me go, turning around to face one of the most stunning women I've ever seen. Long silver hair, pale skin, pale eyes... She's ethereal and lovely in every way. "I didn't know you'd be gracing us with your presence today," she adds, her voice like a cat's purr. She has an accent that I can't quite place.

Marius bends down and kisses both of her cheeks before looking at me. "Graziola, this is Elizabeth. My fiancée."

I swear, Graziola's face shutters for a second before she beams down at me. "So nice to meet the woman who finally tamed the devil," she quips.

"Graziola is the coven leader for the Europe witches," Marius explains, and understanding dawns on me as she looks between us. A knot of jealousy in my stomach hardens, and I grind my jaw. Not my business.

"I see," I say politely.

"Next time I'm in Edinburgh, I must stop by your place so we can catch up."

Marius gives her a half-smile. "As long as it's okay with my wife."

She tilts her head and assesses us once more. "You guys make a great couple. Congratulations. When is the wedding?"

I stiffen, but Marius squeezes my hand once. "This week. It'll be small, but we'll be sure to send word afterward."

A total and complete brush-off. Graziola must realize his insinuation, because her lips press together and she nods once.

"Enjoy your time in Adeñata, Elizabeth." She gives Marius a soft smile. "Goodbye, Marius."

As she walks away, he watches Graziola go. I lift my chin and drop my hand from his, swallowing thickly.

"We should do the rounds," he says quickly, taking my hand again and pulling me behind him.

I'm still ruminating on everything—still thinking of Ciro and Graziola—so I don't answer him as we wander the tunnels casually. I keep my eyes trained on the darkness lurking within the cells, but I don't see anything. They must all be either hidden from me, thanks to Marius, or lurking in the far corners of their cells. My skin cools when I realize it must be the latter.

How the hell did my life go from a normal twenty-year-old to checking up on a Spanish monster prison with my fiancé who also happens to be the *actual* devil? My hands begin to shake as another wave of realization hits me—another wave of loneliness. My chest aches as we finish the tour. Marius glances down at me every minute, probably sensing the change in my energy, but I don't make eye contact. Instead, I just put one foot in front of the other and wait for this day to be over. All I want is to crawl back underneath the covers and sleep forever.

"Elizabeth."

My name on his lips stirs me from my stupor,

and I look around. He'd somehow teleported us to the top of the stairs, or maybe I walked them in my numbed state and didn't realize. The iron door to the arena outside was open. The same black SUV from earlier awaits us on the other side.

"Are we done?"

He nods, his brows furrowed as he studies my face. "We're headed back to one of my houses."

I narrow my eyes. "We're not going back to Edinburgh?"

"Not tonight," he remarks, pulling me into the arena behind him. I hadn't realized how much time we'd spent in the prison. The sun is beginning to set.

"But I didn't bring anything for staying overnight," I whine, feeling tired and hungry and hot.

"I had Annabelle pack you an overnight bag."

"There better be two rooms," I mutter, and we climb into the car together. He closes the door, and I sag with relief as the cool, air-conditioned air hits my sweaty skin. When I look over at him, he's scowling down at his phone. It's the first time I've seen him use technology, aside from the airplane controls. "The devil is an iPhone user," I joke, leaning back against the cool leather.

He frowns as he looks up at me. "Cellphones are ridiculous. Humans are self-destructing with shit like this. Until fifteen years ago, people used to look up at the world. They used to *talk* to people, to their faces, and enjoy their lives. But now? They're addicted, constantly looking down at a piece of flimsy metal."

I smirk. "You sound like a snob."

He sighs and throws his phone onto the seat next to him. "I suddenly live in a world where no one is willing to bare their souls anymore. It's all for show." He looks over at me. "It can be quite lonely."

I swallow. "That does sound lonely." I look down at his phone. "Do you have Twitter?"

He sighs again, but I swear, his lips twitch. "No. I'm merely an observer."

"I see."

The car drives us through the old town of

Adeñata. There are houses I'm sure are at least a thousand years old. The streets are narrow, and the ocean gives the entire city a green-bluish hue, yet the beach and peaked mountains surrounding us are black as night. It's unlike anything I've ever seen. The car stops in front of a small house overlooking the ocean. Even though it's small, the details are intricate and ornate, giving off a vibe of another century. A gold dome sits atop the house, making the whole area feel like we're not even on the same planet as Edinburgh.

Marius helps me out before grabbing our bags from the trunk of the car. Waving the driver goodbye, we head through the front door—something Marius has a key for.

He opens the door, and I look around, noting the terracotta tiled floors, the gilded furniture, and arched doorways. The sun is streaming through the large front window, sending rays of light slicing through the house, if I can even call it that. A large, tiled fountain sits in the center of the room, and beyond it, a decent-sized bed that sits within a dark, wooden bed frame. There's a table, a couple of chairs, and a kitchenette. I glance around, noting the small bathroom off the bedroom area.

"There are no walls," I say, looking at the way the bathroom is simply carved into the wall, like no one bothered to place a door there.

"I never expected to have company," he says, dropping our bags at the foot of the bed. "I'll sleep on the floor."

Without another word, he steps into the bathroom and begins to undress. I turn away, walking over to one of the leather poufs next to the table, ignoring my heated cheeks as the sound of a shower permeates the small space.

Distracting myself, I pull my phone out and turn it on, but no notifications pop up. I blocked the one person who would be worrying where I am, and the other doesn't seem to give a shit anymore. I power it off again, and for the first time since everything happened, I wonder if perhaps being here with Marius isn't the worst thing. After all, I haven't really had time to think about Shepherd and Rachel. I've been too busy wrapping my mind around everything. And if it doesn't matter whether or not I go back to Edinburgh, back to my old life… maybe I could wait this one out and see what happens.

It was better than moping around all alone, that's for sure.

Nine
MARIUS

After drying myself off, I peak around the corner of the shower. Elizabeth is perched uncomfortably at the table, her feet to one side and her arm holding up her head as she looks down at her screen and slams it down on the metal table. Wrapping the towel around my waist, I walk to my bag and pull a pair of sweatpants out, bringing them back to the bathroom to pull on. I don't look to see if she's watching me walk away. I can practically feel the heat radiating off her body, heating this godforsaken house more than it already is.

When I walk back out, she's rummaging

through her bag, making clicking noises with her tongue. She slowly walks to the bathroom, her eyes hanging on mine for a second too long, so I walk to the other side of the room, to give her a small semblance of privacy.

A minute later, she walks back out wearing a linen shirt and short set that leaves very little to the imagination—and I understand why she made those discontented sounds earlier.

"I think Annabelle has an ulterior motive," she grumbles, stuffing her dress and shoes into her bag. She'd undone her braid, instead throwing her hair up on the top of her head. I can't blame her—it's stifling in here.

I let myself laugh for the first time today. "She can be meddlesome, but I think she just knew how hot it was here and packed accordingly."

"Speaking of," Elizabeth says, walking over to one of the windows. "Can I open a window?"

"Go right ahead," I retort, crossing my arms as I watch her attempt to unlatch the Moorish windows.

"How the fuck do these open?" she says through gritted teeth.

Walking up behind her, I push on the top

of the window, and it swivels open. Her mouth drops open.

"These were all the rage when I bought this house," I explain, and her eyes bore into mine.

"And when was that?" she asks, looking around.

"Eight hundred years ago."

Her face pales slightly. I turn around and sit down at the table, and she follows. With a snap of my fingers, two plates and two cups appear, and she gasps.

"Oh my God," she breathes, her voice stirring something dormant inside of me. "What is this?"

"Tortilla de patatas—which is a potato and onion omelet, and pintos—which are bread topped with various items. There's also Pescado Asado a la Vasca, which is a fresh fish—"

She begins to shovel food in her mouth, and I quell the guilt that flashes through me at the thought of her being so hungry. If I'm going to demand she live with me and be my wife, the least I can do is properly feed her.

We both eat in silence, and once her plate starts to clear, I add more food—this time, some sausage, paella, and finally, some Basque cheesecake with a side of chocolate-covered churros. She moans when she sees it, and I adjust myself as my cock throbs inside of my sweats.

A few minutes later, she groans and pushes her plate away. "That was the best food I've ever had," she says slowly, taking a sip of the red wine I poured us earlier.

"I try to make a point of eating the local food when I visit Adeñata," I answer. "And I apologize that this is our first meal since breakfast. From now on, I'll be sure to feed you regularly."

She smirks. "I do tend to get quite hangry," she admits.

I lean back and study her as I sip my wine. Maybe it's the wine—which is my own, potent blend from down south—or maybe it's the fact that the heat is making me feel a bit delirious. But suddenly, I feel lucky that I get to marry such a beautiful woman. I'd only ever met her as a baby—with fiery, red hair in pigtails. Her mother was pretty, but Elizabeth must've inherited some traits from her father, because they don't look that alike. Her mother was very thin, very practical-minded and... plain. Elizabeth is voluptuous—a dreamer with a barbed tongue. Her heart-shaped face and full lips make her seem angelic, but the second she opens her mouth...

"When were you born?" she asks, placing both hands around her wine glass. Her eyes are a bit glazed over—likely from the heat, the wine, and the long day.

"I wasn't born," I admit. "I just was," I say, trying to explain it in a way that she will understand. "I was never human; therefore, I was never born. Monsters and creatures in this world are rarely born. We're just the remnants of what used to rule this earth thousands of years ago—before the humans found ways to kill most of us."

She cocks her head. "So, you've been witness to every great event in history?"

I shrug. "Not exactly. I evolved the same way humans did, so my consciousness does not go back *that* far. If I had to guess, I've been on this earth, in this form, for about fifty thousand years."

Her jaw drops open. "Holy shit. You're like... a relic." Her eyes burn red, and I reach out to cup her chin.

"Most men don't like being called relics, Crimson."

She audibly swallows, and I love how despite how she thinks she feels, her body is my puppet. "Crimson?" she asks, jerking herself away from me.

"Your eyes," I explain, and I make mine burn red, too. "You have my blood, Elizabeth. I can feel my power running through your veins."

She doesn't say anything as her eyes go back to their normal ochre color as they sweep over my face. "Did you mean it when you said we would be getting married this week?"

I clench my jaw. "Yes." Something akin to disappointment passes over her face, and she continues, "Why the rush to marry? Couldn't we like... get to know each other for a few months?"

She's *so* young. If only it were that easy. "We must marry, because in my culture, marriage entails a combining of blood."

She stills, and I see the realization hit her.

"So, the whole reason you're marrying me is so that you have access to my blood?" she says softly.

"When I made the bargain with your mother, I gave you my blood—to heal you. For my power to return fully, you must uphold your end of the deal, Elizabeth."

Her lips flatten, and her eyes flash red again. "So, all you want is your power?"

I chuckle, and her nostrils flare as she clenches her jaw. "No. All I want is for us to share all the power. Once we marry, our blood will become one, and you will become just as powerful as I am. I also want to protect you, because whether you believe it or not, people already suspect what you are, and they will stop at nothing to use that power to do terrible things, or worse, to harm you. You are safest with me—by my side as my wife, sharing my blood," I growl.

Her lip wobbles a bit before she lifts her chin and clears her throat. "You said yesterday that I took too much blood when you healed me. What did you mean?"

The corner of my lips lifts into a small

smile. "It means that even as a two-year-old, you were conniving and devious. It means that once we are married, our power balance will be restored—and no one can harm either of us if we're together."

She rears her head back. "It's hard to believe that a *lowly fae* is the key to your survival considering you're fifty thousand years old," she quips, her eyes crinkling at the use of Ciro's words from earlier.

I smirk, reaching out and running a finger down her jaw. "You're right. Except, when your mother made that blood bond with me, she also unknowingly formed a mating bond between you and me."

Ten
LIZ

I MAY ONLY HAVE KNOWN ABOUT BEING FAE FOR A day, but even I know what a mating bond is.

Two people connected by some higher power. My friends and I called them soulmates, and in the books I read, they were usually sparked by some intense eye contact and perhaps some biting or smut. But in real life? I stare at the man before me—the man who rules over dangerous monsters, who rules over purgatory for humans, who is *thousands* of years old… and I'm supposed to be his mate?

I suddenly feel self-conscious.

Between Graziola and the *millions* of other

women he's been with in the last fifty millennia, how am I ever supposed to compare to them? I've only ever been with one man, and we never did anything weird—it was straight, vanilla sex. Marius must be able to read my expression, because he drops his gaze to my chest.

"Elizabeth," he purrs, resting his arms on his knees. "Say something."

I shake my head. "I-I'm just trying to wrap my brain around everything." My chest feels tight again, and I rub my neck and take a few calming breaths. "I know what a mating bond is, I'm just—" I bite my lower lip. "What does it mean for *us*?" I ask, my body tense.

His eyes blaze red for a second, and then he leans in closer. "It means that we will be one soul in two bodies," he murmurs. "It means that we can read each other's minds, and that my pleasure is yours, and vice versa," he whispers. "It means when we fuck, we might very well cause mountains to crumble, and entire cities to burn," he purrs.

My core tightens, and my clit throbs at his words, sending electric currents shooting down my legs. I feel my nipples harden beneath my linen camisole, and my pulse pounds against every inch of my skin.

Before I can even attempt to come up with a response to that, he stands up and reaches his hand out to me.

"We should get some sleep," he says, and I let him pull me up with effortless ease.

"Sure," I mumble, not sure I can form words.

I walk into the bathroom and brush my teeth, quickly washing my face and using the luxurious face lotion that Annabelle packed for me. I keep the water running at full speed as I pee—*this fucking room really needs a door*. After I brush out my hair, I leave it cascading down my back and exit the bathroom. I stop walking when I see Marius curled up on the stone floor, a flimsy blanket barely covering his body.

"Do you need the bathroom?" I ask, gesturing to where I just exited.

Marius rolls over to his back and places his hands behind his head as he gives me a small, mischievous smile. "Magic," he says, and I get a whiff of mint.

"Are you comfortable there?" I ask, not sure why I'm choosing to be accommodating to the man who is demanding that I marry him.

"I'll be fine," he says smoothly. He turns over and the blanket comes off his back. He shimmies underneath it, his knees practically to his chest. He doesn't even have a proper pillow, just his overnight bag.

I sigh. "Get in the bed, Marius."

"I'm fine," he murmurs, closing his eyes just as the lights wink out. *Magic.*

"I won't be able to sleep if I know I made the devil sleep on the floor."

He chuckles and then he stands up and pads closer. "I promise not to bite."

I don't answer him as I crawl to the very edge of the bed, turning away from the center. I am used to sleeping in the same room as strange men—Rachel and I used to backpack all over the United Kingdom. We'd oftentimes be the only two women in a room full of men. This is just like that.

Except those men weren't extremely attractive, wise, devious men with horns and a tail.

"Go to sleep, Elizabeth. I can practically hear your anxious wheels turning."

I pull the covers over myself and try to go to sleep, but my body is so aware of every breath Marius takes. I don't feel sleepy like I did earlier, instead, I feel jittery and uptight. I think of all the things I want to say to Rachel and Shepherd the next time I see them. I think of my mother, who was so consumed in another world at the end that I can't help but believe this whole farce. She spoke of other worlds, of faeries and witches. I thought it was just Alzheimer's, but now I know she was just letting her guard down. And my father? Who was he? Was he still alive, and did he know my mother was a fae?

"Elizabeth," Marius growls.

"I can't sleep," I admit, biting my thumb nail. Whether he likes it or not, by being the only person I have to talk to, he's privy to my distressed and cluttered thoughts. He doesn't respond, but I can sense his body roll over to face me. I keep my back to him. "What was my mother like?" I ask, my voice smaller than I intended.

He's quiet for a few seconds, like he's mulling over his words. "She was scared," he says honestly. "There was real fear in her eyes, and she had these dark bags under them. I don't think she'd eaten in days—the bones in her chest were protruding," he continues slowly. "She was fae, so she knew about me. Only desperate people find me, Elizabeth. I knew she was going to sacrifice her life to save you. But I didn't want you to grow up motherless. So, to save her the trouble, I asked for you outright."

I swallow, and my eyes prick with tears.

"I knew back then that our blood had mixed, and that somehow, the mixing had formed the mating bond. I figured you'd come of age, and we could figure it out together at that point. I never expected her to glamour you. And it infuriated me, because you were *mine*," he growls, sending shivers down my spine.

Something slithers against the back of my thighs, and I freeze, my breath caught in my throat. It's too large to be his cock, right? There's no way… and *why* would he do that, anyway?

"What—"

"Open your legs."

His command sends heat flaring through me. It's so intense that my core physically *aches* for him, and I do as I'm told, lifting my right knee slightly.

Whatever slithered against my thighs now slithers between my legs, feeling me, caressing me.

Holy Gods. It's his tail.

I stiffen at the realization, but it feels too good to tell him to stop. The end is barbed, coarse, but the actual length of his tail is smooth, large, and warm. It curves up, and the barb comes to my chest, resting against my scar. I have to will my hips not to freaking hump his tail.

What the hell is wrong with me?

"In a few days, we will be married and mated," Marius purrs. "I'm not going to fuck you until after we've taken our vows, because I've had my fair share of mediocre sex," he murmurs.

"Me too," I admit, the words more like a moan than anything else.

He uses that to his benefit, pressing his tail hard against my body and bringing the barb lower and lower, grazing my exposed stomach. I let out a low moan, and Marius growls with satisfaction. I reach down and feel for his tail, and it shudders against my hand as I touch it.

"Be careful with that," Marius hisses from behind me. "I treat my tail like a second cock."

His words burn through me, and my clit pulses. I clench involuntarily, feeling the way the barbs are like thick fingers—each one twice the width of a normal finger, and maybe a few inches longer. *Fuck.* I roll my hips as the barbed ends curve and make their way under the waistband of my shorts. Marius grunts behind me.

"You're wet for me, Crimson," he declares, the coarse barbs sliding against my slickness. "I want you to melt under my touch, Elizabeth." He inserts one barb, and I gasp as it fills and stretches me slowly. "I want you to leak my come for days," he purrs, thrusting the barb further into me while another one circles my clit.

Oh, fuck. Of course, the devil is a supreme dirty talker.

I writhe under his touch, and he inserts another barb, making me cry out. I'm just about to ask him to stop when he flips me smoothly onto my stomach, the length of his tail lifting my hips. The barbs don't move, and at this angle, I feel him come behind me. I try to shove him away, but he grabs my hands as he drives the barbed end of his tail in and out of me, but instead of one of the barbs circling my clit, the smooth part of his tail presses against me, making my pussy grip the barbs.

"Good girl," Marius growls. He let go of my hands to reach around to my breasts, squeezing them. *Holy fuck.* I cry out and arch my back against him, and he presses his hard cock against my ass.

Double fuck, it's massive.

I throw my head back, and he bends down, his breath tickling the top of my ear.

"You're letting me fuck you with my tail before I even kiss you," he murmurs, squeezing my nipples and rolling them between his thumb and forefinger. "I wasn't sure what you would be like when I tore the world apart, Elizabeth, but if I knew that, I might've tried a little harder," he purrs, nipping at my ear.

A wave of pleasure unlike anything I've ever known passes through me, and I arch my back, stiffening as my pussy contracts around his thick barbs. My wetness lubricates the smooth slickness of his tail, and I full-on ride his tail, squirming against it as I cry out, as my toes curl, as my nipples throb under Marius's calloused fingers. The room spins as my climax begins, and I fuck his tail hard as his long tongue licks the side of my neck, sending another cascade of overpowering heat and bliss through my veins.

"Come on my tail," Marius commands, his voice hoarse. "I want to be dripping with your come, Elizabeth." He must be controlling the waves of pleasure, because the sensation gets stronger and stronger until I'm screaming, until a throbbing pressure sits in my lower abdomen. I'm sure I'm going to pee, and I pause for a second. Marius grips my wrist.

"I said, come on my tail, Elizabeth," he grits out. "Give me *everything*, Crimson. Don't hold back."

I do as he says and relax my pelvis, and what happens next only intensifies everything into the most earth-shattering feeling I've ever experienced. My pussy grips him, milking his barbs, making him groan and thrust into my ass as wave after wave hits me. My body twitches as I spray the bed, his tail, and his hand that grips the inside of my thigh before collapsing back onto the bed.

"Fuck yes," he growls. His tail comes out from underneath me, retracting back and leaving me feeling empty and sore.

Marius lays down next to me, and I get a glimpse of the wet spot in his shorts. Raising my eyebrows, I smirk.

"Can you…" I trail off, looking behind him where his tail must've disappeared.

"Come without touching? Yes. I wasn't joking when I said it's like a second cock. When I fuck things with it, I come—and I come hard."

He grabs my hand and places it on top of his hard bulge. My clit throbs needily when I feel the huge mess he made.

"Look what you did to me, Elizabeth," he purrs, and his cock bobs at my touch. "I came twice, actually."

I sit up and look down at him, and *fuck me* if I wasn't already willing to go for round two. I'm just about to ask when he gives me a cocky smile.

"I wasn't joking when I said I wanted to wait to fuck you until after we married and mated."

"But why—"

"Because that?" he says slowly, sitting up and pressing me back down into the bed. Pinning my wrists at my side, he licks my neck again before dragging his tongue lower. "That was nothing compared to mated sex."

I see stars as his tongue roves downward. "How am I supposed to sleep now?"

Marius's resounding chuckle tickles the skin on my hip, and then he moves my waistband down, gazing down at my bare pussy.

"I think the real question is, how am *I* supposed to sleep with this perfect rosebud of a cunt a mere two feet away?" And then he slides his tongue between my slit, slurping vulgarly. "Fuck, Elizabeth. You taste so fucking good. I could eat your pussy for *days* on end."

I arch my back as his tongue—longer than a human tongue—sweeps up and down, not missing an inch of nerves. He alternates between up and down and side to side, sucking my clit and adding spit for lube. It's the hottest and dirtiest thing I've ever done.

"I haven't had enough," he murmurs against my skin, and just then, I feel his tail snake under his body, driving into me with such force that my head hits the headboard. "I need another release, or my cock will be hard all night."

Holy fuck.

He inserts a third barb, and this time, I let them stretch me. I let them fill and fuck me, the coarseness intensifying everything. Marius moans, writhing, as he eats my pussy, and I squeeze my eyes shut as waves of pleasure flash through me, down to the tips of my toes. I cry out, gripping the sheets with one hand and Marius's hair with the other, fucking his mouth, *loving* the rough feeling of his scruff against my vulva. I roll my hips and his hands hold me still as his tail drives in and out of me.

"Oh fuck," he grunts. "Eo venire tam difficile stupri. Ita stupri infectum es. Numquam ego satis," he grits out against my swollen cunt. *He's speaking Latin.*

"God," I cry out. "Harder!"

He lifts his head so that he's looking down at me, looking at the way his tail thrusts in and out of me. Then he removes it, the barbs dripping with my come, and pulls his sweatpants down.

"I just need a taste," he murmurs, sliding

his shaft between my folds. He isn't penetrating me—not technically.

"I thought you said you wanted to wait," I whisper, my words caught in my throat.

He gives me a lopsided smile. "This is why they didn't make me an angel." And then he grips my hips with his hand and glides between the lips of my pussy. *Hard.*

"Oh my God," I whimper, the feel of his large, warm cock against my clit sending the first wave of an orgasm through me. I shake and shudder underneath him, screaming his name over and over. The sounds of my wetness permeate the air, but I don't even care.

Marius's jaw clenches and his cock begins to pulse. He stops his movement, instead letting it sit inside of my cleft as spurt after spurt of come covers my abdomen. He just hisses, grabbing my hips and letting himself empty on top of me. Even though he didn't penetrate me, it feels like the hottest sex I've ever had, and my whole body is tingling and sore all at once.

He pulls away and walks into the bathroom naked, his ass firm and muscular as he walks. He grabs a towel and wipes me down, and then he helps me up without saying anything. I feel drowsy, and he must notice because he gives me privacy to use the toilet, and then we take a quick shower. Together.

It doesn't even feel weird.

A minute later, I crawl into bed, my body limp and throbbing with pain. I didn't realize just how rough he was, and I'm sure tomorrow, I'll be riddled with bruises. He crawls in behind me, a warm hand coming to the top of my chest. I sense him sending some sort of healing, calming power through me.

"Why didn't you do that earlier?" I ask, my voice thick with sleep. "When I was having trouble sleeping?"

"Because I really wanted to fuck you, Elizabeth. Now, go to sleep. For real this time."

I'm out before he finishes speaking.

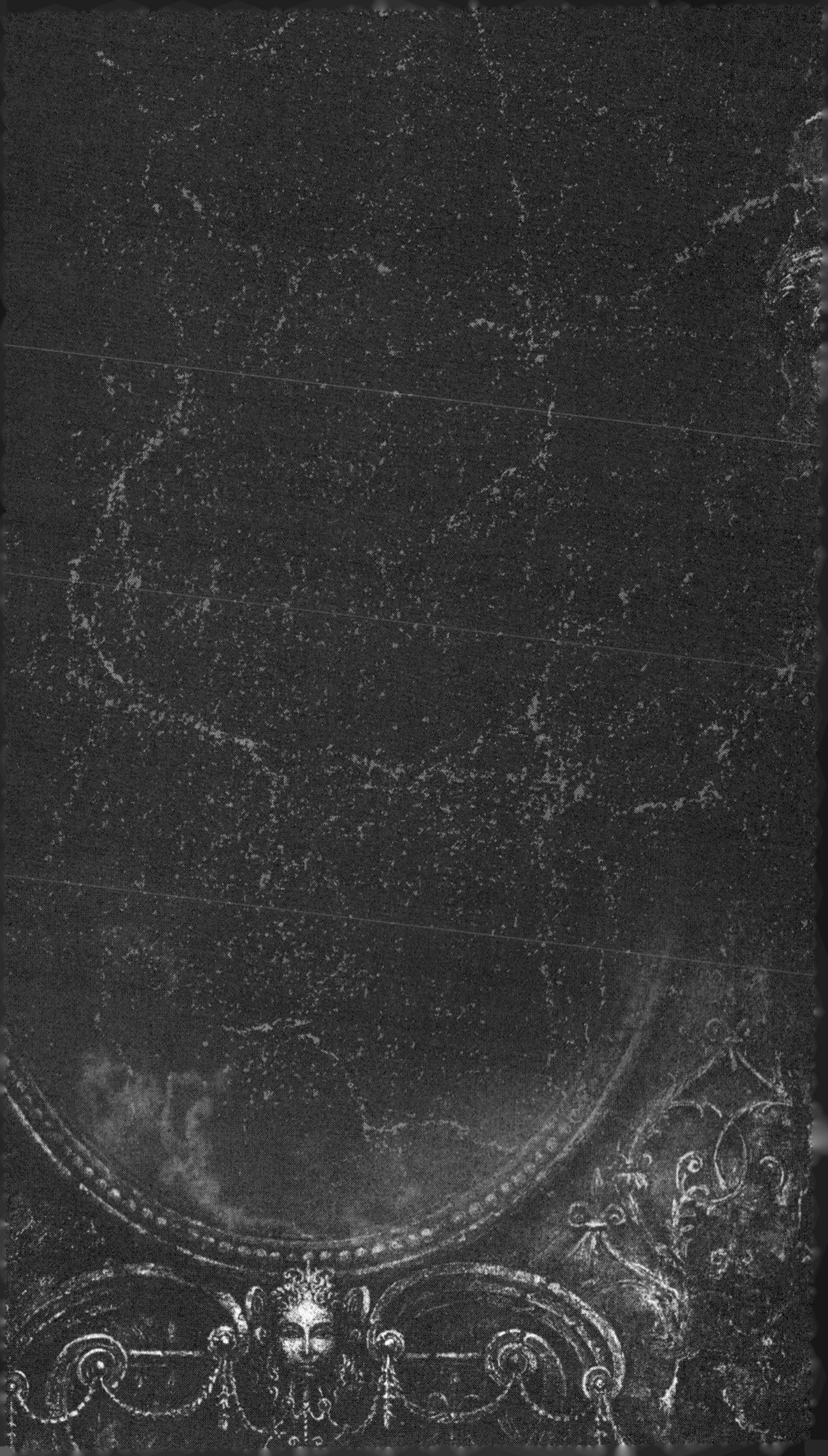

Eleven
LIZ

We fly back to Edinburgh the next morning—after a quick romp in the shower, that is. Marius on his knees before me, feasting on me and worshiping me… it does something to my insides. I'm not sure if the mating bond has somehow snapped into place, or if I'm just so broken that I'll accept any form of love and attention he throws my way, but I can't get enough.

After we land, we take a car back to his castle, and I settle into the leather seat. Watching my city go by, a strange sense of calm overcomes me. In a way, not having to find a new job, not having to renew the lease on my flat, and not having to inevitably see Rachel or Shepherd around town—in exchange for becoming Marius' wife—is something I'm more than willing to do. I don't have the capacity to think or digest everything that's happened, so the next best thing is being cared for by someone who seems to have my best interests at heart.

Once we're back, Annabelle greets us at the front door, and then she whisks me away to my very first magic lesson, something Marius insists I do. So that's how I spend my days, training my mind, learning to control my magic, and then crawling into Marius's bed at night and letting him devour me with his mouth or his tail. I learn that I'm powerful but untrained… it could be dangerous for me and everyone around me. My magic is raw and fueled by my emotions, so my eyes burn red, and my hands turn to flames whenever I get angry. I also discovered that sadness brings about frost—as I so inconveniently discovered one morning after Marius had left the bed. The duvet? It had turned to pure ice, and I needed Annabelle's help to get out from underneath it.

The wedding is set for this Saturday, exactly one week after meeting Marius at Dante's Inferno. He tells me I can invite whoever I want, but the only person I insist on being there is Rory. To distract Marius from the look of pity on his face when I tell him that, I drop to my knees and pull his already hard cock into my mouth. I do change my status to engaged on Facebook, connecting my profile with his anonymous profile. It fills me with glee to think about Rachel and Shepherd wondering who Marius Hadriana Lucius de Augustus XVII is. And yes, that's his full name, having accrued a few different surnames over the years.

When I'm not attending my magic lessons or in bed with Marius, I'm pestering him with questions about Rome, Constantinople, Ancient China, Mesopotamia, Jesus, and the World Wars. I didn't realize he'd fought nearly every single war, including World War II. There's even a picture of him on the beaches of Normandy. He's had a hand in every major historical event in modern history. When I decide to tease him and ask how big the dinosaurs were, he just throws me down on the floor of the dining room and punishes me with his hand.

The day before the wedding, Annabelle flies a designer from London up to Edinburgh, and I get to try on the dress I didn't realize she'd picked out for me. It's stunning, with creme lace fabric that's fitted up top, coming off the shoulders. It's skintight until my knees and then it flares out. It fits me like a glove, and I love the way it sits snugly against my skin yet allows me to move around freely. It's exactly the kind of thing I would've picked out for myself.

Marius isn't present at dinner, but Rory is, and we spend three hours drinking as we cackle and attempt to turn the candlesticks into dildos. After Rory leaves, I turn to face Annabelle.

"Where is my future husband?" The words tumble out easily after the strong wine Rory and I had with our food.

She smirks. "He's in his room, but I'm under strict orders not to let you in."

My brows furrow. "Why?"

"Because he's very traditional, and he doesn't want to see you until the wedding tomorrow."

I cross my arms. "The devil has morals?"

She chuckles. "You need your sleep."

I frown and twist around, heading up the stairs. "Fine." I sigh.

"I ran you a bath," she calls up to me, and I can't help but smile as I wander into my room and close the door.

As much as I want to go bother Marius, it might be better if we spend tonight apart. After all, he has promised me nothing but sex tomorrow night, and I have a feeling I'm going to need to catch up on sleep tonight because of it. I shimmy out of my clothes and step into the steaming water. Somehow, Annabelle always seems to know exactly what I need. My body is sore from being handled by Marius, and even though he doesn't mean to hurt me, I am mortal, and he is immortal. Even just the simple act of grabbing my hips in the middle of using his tail leaves bruises along my skin, especially if he's not paying attention to how rough he's being.

I slip deeper into the water, letting the bubbles come up to my chin. I haven't looked at my phone in days, except to change my Facebook status. It's a weird feeling, leaving everything behind for this new life. Walking away from my friend, my ex, my job, my apartment… and everything I had ever known. On one hand, I wish I could talk to my mom about it. But on the other hand, I can't help but be a little mad at her for making the blood bargain in the first place. If nothing else, I wish she'd warned me about Marius.

I close my eyes and lean my head back, feeling my body floating and completely weightless in the large tub. In the last few days, I've given up hope that there's a way out of this blood bargain. Even if there was, would I want to leave the luxury of this castle? Would I want to leave Annabelle and Rory, two people who are fast becoming friends? And would I want to leave Marius?

Marius… with the crinkles around his eyes when he laughs.

With the strong forearms that can lift and throw me around with ease.

With the never-ending stories, the infinite number of firsthand accounts throughout history.

And tomorrow, I get to marry him.

I wash myself quickly, feeling my eyes

getting heavy. Changing into a negligee, I brush my teeth before climbing into bed, where I drift off to the faraway sound of classical music coming from Marius's bedroom.

※

I wake up in a panic, my eyes finding the early morning light beginning to creep through the slits of my bedroom window curtains. I throw the covers off and grab a sweater, slipping my feet into my felt mules. I grab my phone and wrap my arms around myself as I creep down the stairs, tiptoeing across the creaky, old wood of the living room. Entering the kitchen, I grab a glass of water and sit down at the breakfast nook, powering it on.

I'm not even sure what the point is—Marius decided my fate a week ago, and I'm basically stuck here. Not that I want to leave. I've come to like his long tongue, and the way he seems to look at me with reverence. But I guess I need to check one last time if Shepherd or Rachel have reached out. I need closure, even though I know I'm better off now.

Text messages ping as soon as I pick up

service, and I swipe my phone open to read them.

Shepherd: You're *engaged*?

Shepherd: Liz, talk to me. What's going on?

Shepherd: Rachel and I are done. I told her it was a mistake. I want you back, Lizzie. Please call me.

Shepherd: Where the fuck are you? I've been knocking for hours, and you haven't come home.

Shepherd: Did you forget that you shared your location with me? It says you're in the middle of fucking nowhere.

Shepherd: What the fuck, Liz?

Shepherd: Are you okay? Now I'm worried you're lying in a ditch somewhere.

Shepherd: Fuck it. I'm coming for you.

My heart jumps to my throat when I see he sent the last text two hours ago. I stand up and look around. Realistically, he's not even going to be able to see this place. It's glamoured so that humans can't lay eyes on it. Still, my skin pebbles with unease. I slip out of my mules and walk to the foyer, where I grab a pair of wellies and slip them on. Opening the front door, I step out into the cold, misty morning.

I walk along the curved driveway, taking in the soft, pink glow of the sky, and the way the fog seems to lay across the bright green lawn. I tromp through it, walking to the open meadow in front of the castle so that I can see if Shepherd is even here, or if he somehow got past the glamour. I turn the corner of the stone wall, and the vision before me stops me in my tracks.

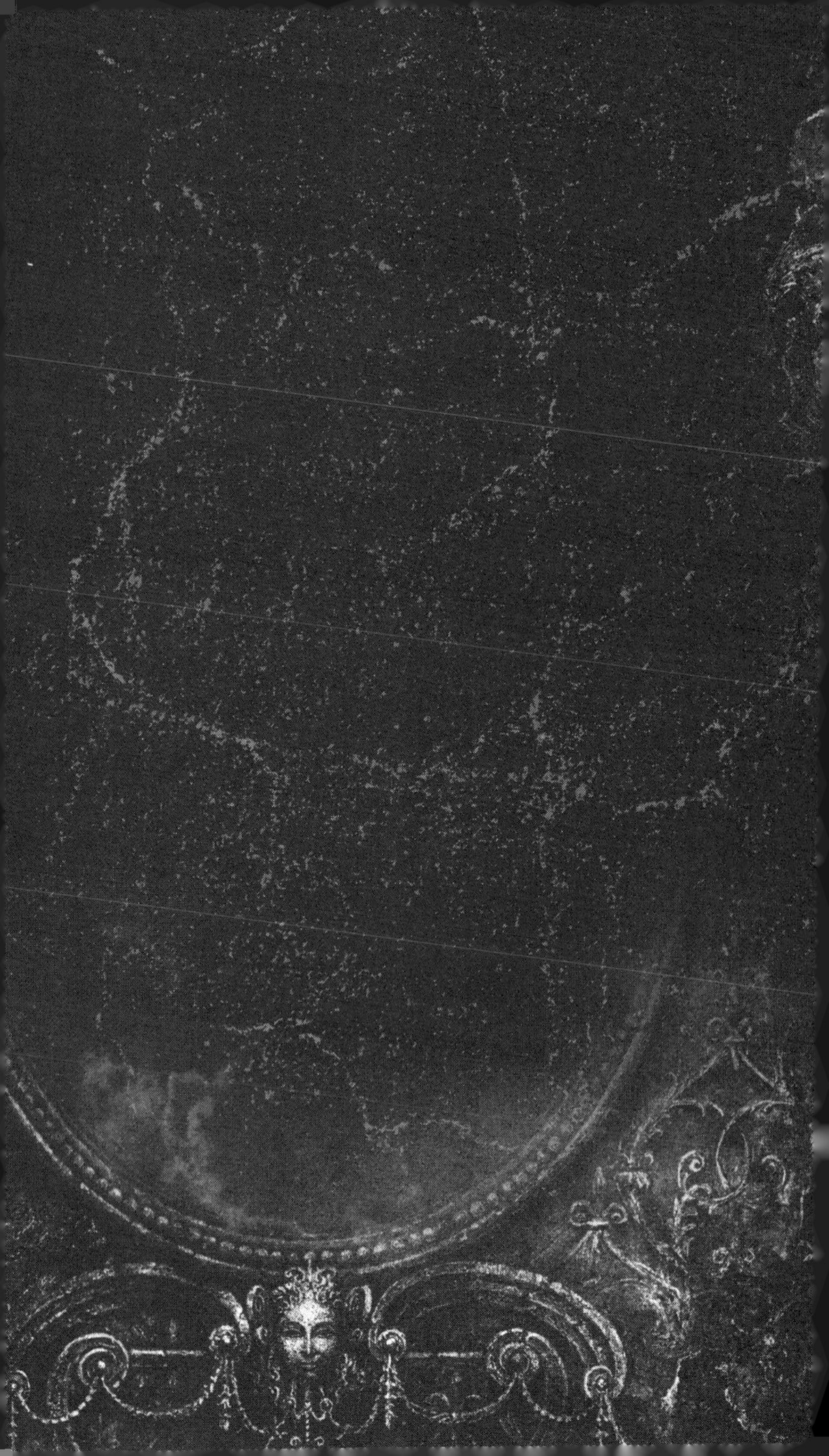

Twelve
MARIUS

Elizabeth walks around the corner just as I whip my knife out, holding it at this bastard's throat.

"What the hell are you doing?" At first, I think she's asking this idiot what he's doing, trespassing and insisting he knows her. *My* Elizabeth. But then her eyes find mine, and they're wide and pleading. "Marius, what are you doing?"

"Liz," the barbarian croaks, flailing in my arms. He's putty—skin and bones and flesh. *So easy to break, to maim.*

The beast inside of me roars to life, and I

press down harder on his neck.

Hard enough to draw blood.

"Stop, you're hurting him," Elizabeth cries, running forward. "This... He's my ex-boyfriend," she explains.

Disappointment rolls through me. I thought for sure that he was just some power-hungry human here to seek her out. There'd been a few supernaturals sniffing around the castle this week. Sending a human in their wake to do their dirty work wouldn't surprise me.

"What the fuck is going on, Liz," the human huffs, and I grit my teeth.

"Shut up, or I'll slide your head off in one motion."

Looking up at Elizabeth, I find her eyes are glazed over with fear... and horror. The same look she had the first night we met.

I swallow. I am a monster, through and through. I am forcing her to marry me. Surely, Elizabeth—this sweet, innocent, marvelous woman—deserves better than me?

"Let him go," she pleads, walking closer. "Marius. Let. Him. Go." Her eyes burn red, and she reaches out for my hand. "Please."

The instant I drop the knife, the air changes, and before I have time to process it, the human elbows me in the nose, sending me to my knees, and then his eyes burn bright green as he lunges forward, tackling Elizabeth to the ground, and sinking his sharp fangs into her neck.

Thirteen
LIZ

The air leaves my lungs as I'm pushed onto my back, and nothing escapes my lips when I see Shepherd mounting me from above, his eyes green, his teeth sharp, and his skin? Bumpy, with pustules and warts covering the surface.

What the actual *fuck?*

Before I can process anything, he bends down, and I feel a sharp prick at the side of my neck. Crying out, I try to shove him off, but he's too big, too strong. I hear him gulping my blood, making little noises of satisfaction, his hand coming up the inside of my thigh—

I'm thrown to the side, but not because

anyone pushed me.

Because Marius tackled Shepherd, and I went with him.

I place a hand on my neck where the warm liquid begins to gush. The world sways before me as my vision tilts. I lost too much blood, but I don't have time to worry about that now. A few feet away, I hear Marius and Shepherd grunting, and when I turn my head, Marius's tail is swinging at Shepherd, the barbed end now sharp as a razor. Shepherd is too quick though, and he leaps up onto his feet and tackles Marius right in the middle. Marius's eyes glow as he falls, and they battle it out on the ground as I try not to pass out.

I press on the wound on my neck, feeling the blood run between my fingers. *Oh, God.* I close my eyes and try to remember what I learned this week with Kline, the small goblin Marius hired to teach me the basics. I visualize the magic flowing from my heart and into my hand, healing the puncture marks. I'll know it's working when my hand warms, or when I stop bleeding. I open my eyes and multi-task—keeping an eye on Marius while also ensuring I don't bleed out. Taking a few calming breaths, I try again. This time, I feel the telltale warmth in my fingertips, and the burning sensation begins to fade. I crawl back a few more feet to the wall, where I hoist myself up so that I can help Marius somehow.

Shepherd turns to me as Marius has him in a headlock. A long, black tongue slithers out of his mouth, and I recoil.

"I knew it," he hisses, his voice wickedly raspy. "I *knew* I could smell his blood in your veins," he adds, grinning at me with pointy teeth. My eyes wander to Marius, and he gives me a knowing smile.

"What are you?" I ask, taking a step closer. I'm still woozy, but every second that passes is a second my healing powers are doing their job.

He cackles, the sound clawing down my spine and making me break into a cold sweat. "Lizzie," he says, his voice soft yet wicked. His large eyes are no longer the blue color I'm so familiar with. They're black, and they bore right into me.

"Don't say my name," I retort, and Marius tightens his grip around Shepherd's neck. I laugh then, the sound escaping my lips as I run my fingers through my hair. "You don't get to say my name. Not now, not ever," I hiss. "You betrayed me, and now I find out that you're this… monster?" I ask, my voice breaking. Marius's eyes find mine, and he gives me a small nod of understanding.

"Lizzie," Shepherd bleats again. "Come on. You love me. I was there. I held your mother's hand as she died," he croaks, his black eyes widening.

I grimace, the memory slamming into me. "I know," I say softly. "But then you fucked Rachel. I could've dealt with this," I say, tears pricking at my eyes. "I could've handled you being whatever the fuck you are," I grit out. "But I can't forgive the betrayal of the heart."

Shepherd scoffs. "I'm sorry, Liz. Forgive me. Please," he begs, and I swear I see a tiny speck of remorse on his distorted face.

I stand taller, looking at Marius. Giving him a small nod, some kind of understanding passes through us, and Shepherd's eyes widen with fear.

"Don't do this, Lizzie. You don't know who

he is," he says.

Marius tightens his grip. "She knows exactly who I am," he purrs, his eyes finding mine and burning as bright as the sun. "I am the King of the Underworld. And you were stupid enough to challenge me."

In one motion, Marius twists Shepherd's neck, and that sends him to the ground in a heap.

"What—" I say, too stunned to finish the sentence.

But it doesn't matter, because the sound of bones regrowing permeates the air, halfway between cracking knuckles and walking through mud. I wince just as Shepherd bounces back up.

"Yeah, thought so," Marius says, his voice bored as he looks down at his nails.

In one swift motion, his tail comes around his hips and pierces Shepherd's chest—the razor-like barb pulling away with a beating, black heart still attached.

I gag, nearly vomiting onto the grass as Shepherd falls, turning to dust immediately after. Marius runs over to me, inspecting every inch.

"Is your neck okay?" he asks, running his thumb over what I'm sure are now just scars.

I nod. "I healed it," I admit. "You were kind of getting your ass kicked, so—"

He tugs me forward and into his arms before I can finish my sentence. Kissing the top of my head, he holds me close, swaying as the mist slowly dissipates in the morning sun.

"I'm sorry," he murmurs.

I shake my head. "I had no idea…" Trailing off, I think of all the times Shepherd and I did human things, like donate blood, go kayaking, bake cookies… and it turns out he was a fucking monster this whole time?!

"He likely sought you out because he was a powerful hybrid. From the smell of his blood, I'd say vampire-monster."

I nod against his warm chest. "Explains why he bit me," I answer.

He chuckles. "And why the glamour on the house didn't work for him. Your mother placed a glamour on you, but he was drawn to you because he could sense it—seeing as vampires are able to sniff out blood way better than any other creature."

"What about Rachel?" I ask, swallowing as the events of the last few minutes rush through me. I begin to tremble in his arms. I'd talked to him about Rachel more than anyone else. I missed her, but I could never forgive what she did.

"It's likely that Rachel is just as powerful as Shepherd, if not more," he murmurs. I hear him reciting some sort of spell. Probably to expand the wards on the house and make it so that paranormal beasts won't be able to just roam around, hunting for me. "We will deal with her later, Elizabeth. For now, let's get inside."

He leads us away toward the house, and I can't help but glance back at the patch of grass where Shepherd disintegrated. Every trace of him is gone. I shiver, and Marius stops walking. He turns to face me, placing his hands on either side of my face.

"Elizabeth, you need to know what you're getting into," he purrs. "I am not a human. I am not fae, like you. I am not gentle, and I do not heal. I exist to kill. I exist to torture and punish. My whole purpose is to ensure people *suffer*," he adds, his voice cracking. "I need to know if you're okay with that. Because if you're not… then I cannot in good conscience marry you."

I swallow, then look up into his brown eyes. Reaching up, I place a hand on his cheek. "You're my Hades," I whisper. "And I'm your Persephone."

Then I reach around to his neck and pull him down for a kiss—our first, true, romantic kiss. Sure, tails are nice, but the way his calloused hand roves up to my hair, fisting it, and the way his other hand comes to my waist, pulling me into him…

I moan into his mouth.

Not because I'm turned on, but because this is the best kiss I've ever experienced. His tongue sweeps into my mouth, and I reach up with both hands, running them through his dark, thick hair. Pulling away, I catch my breath for a few seconds. His lips are red and glistening, and his eyes burn into mine. They're not a fire red, but for the amount of intensity, they may as well be.

"You're sure?" he asks again.

I smile, shrugging casually. "I have tasted the forbidden fruit, Marius. How could I possibly go back now?"

His answering grin is everything I never knew I needed.

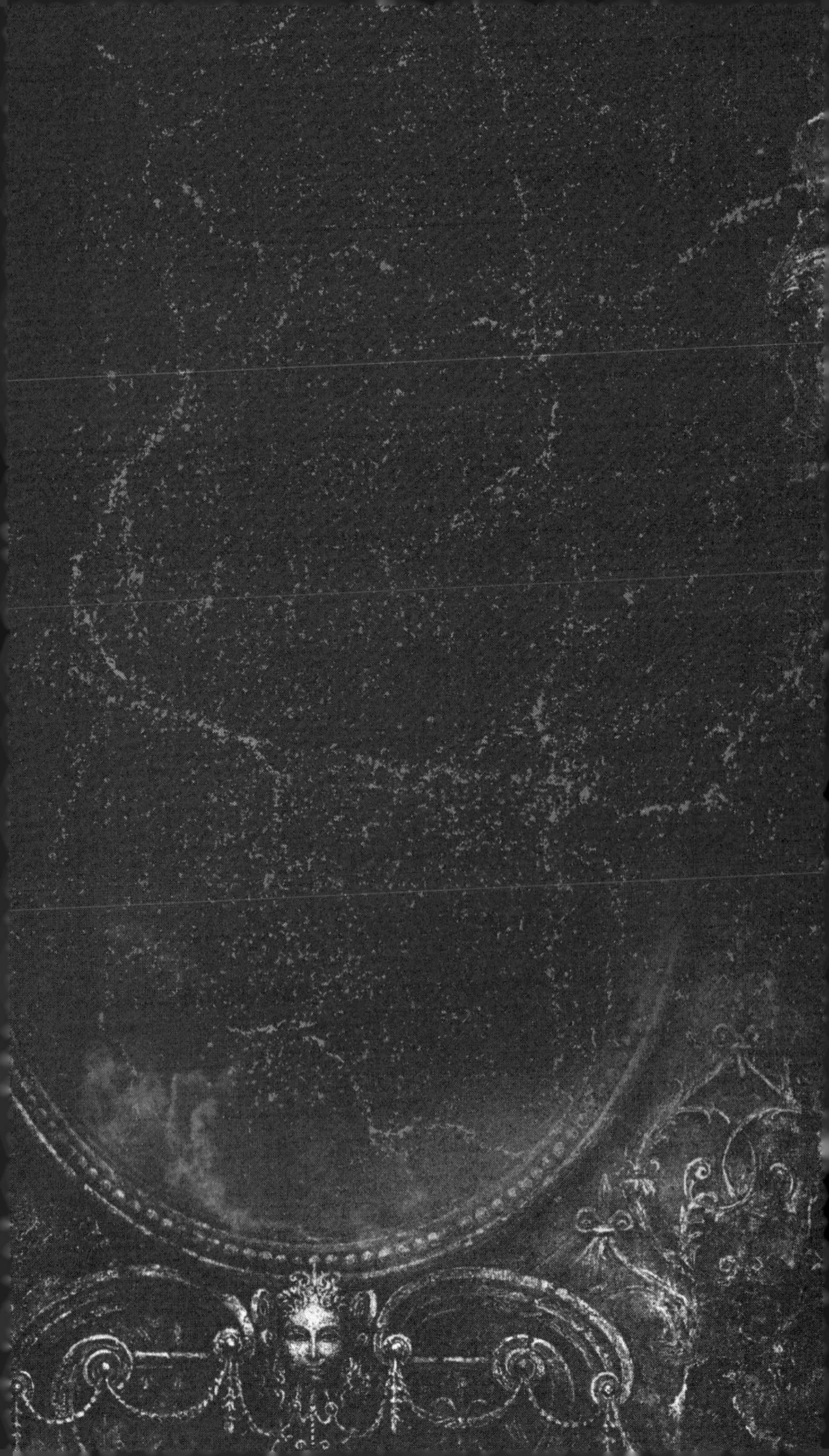

Fourteen
LIZ

The ceremony is small, with only Annabelle and her partner Petra, Rory, Kline, and Marius's valet, George. Annabelle has gone above and beyond in such a short amount of time, and the way she's decorated the chapel is incredible. Twinkling lights—hundreds of them—all line the walls and ceilings. Black roses contrast against the light stone, and as I carry my bouquet of black peonies, I smile at Annabelle, giving her and Petra a nod of appreciation.

Marius cries briefly when he sees me in the dress for the first time, and I have to stifle a laugh at the thought of making the devil cry on our wedding day. We recite traditional vows, and then we perform a blood rite, where we drink each other's blood. It's supposed to restore the power balance, ensuring we're equally powerful, and it also ignites the mating bond. I didn't actually know that last fact, and only suspected it when I had this underlying urge to mount him in front of all our friends.

The warmth of the mating bond snapping into place is a welcome one, and I suddenly understand what people mean when they talk about the mating bond. I have to control myself all through the reception, the long-ass dinner, and then the cutting of the cake. With every wicked gleam in Marius's eyes, my panties get wetter, and by the time we escape the celebrations for our bedroom, I'm already ripping my bodice off before we even get inside the door.

Annabelle had my things moved to his bedroom earlier, so my eyes flick over my belongings approvingly as he backs me up against the bed.

Marius unbuttons his shirt as he prowls

toward me. "I must warn you, Crimson," he growls, pulling my dress down my body. "I don't know if I can be gentle tonight."

Heat flares through me. "I don't want you to be gentle," I answer, my voice low.

That must be the only answer he needs from me, because in one movement, he twists me around and throws me onto the bed. He moves with preternatural speed, pulling my hips up to his as the sound of tearing fabric hits my ears. I look behind me, and my breath is nearly knocked out of me. In place of the human-looking man I just married, kneels the devil—black horns, long tail, red eyes, and a cock big enough to stretch me to the brink. My mouth goes dry as I take in his chiseled abdomen, and the way his large hand strokes his veiny shaft.

I open my mouth to comment on his appearance, but before I can utter the words, he takes one of his hands and shoves my face down onto the duvet, his other hand coming to my hip and rocking me back. His cock impales me, and I cry out in pain as the feel of him expanding inside of me sends a searing sensation through me.

"Elizabeth," he murmurs, his hand moving up my abdomen to brush the underside of my breast. "Just breathe," he purrs. "Deep breaths," he says gently, and I fist the blanket underneath me, closing my eyes. "I should've mentioned that when supernatural creatures mate, the male often knots the female," he growls. I can feel myself expand to meet his girth.

"What does that mean?" I whimper, waiting for the pain to subside.

He bends down and licks my neck, sending tendrils of pleasure through me and eliciting a sultry moan from me. "It means my cock will lock inside of you after I come. There will be no letting you go," he adds, his voice low and rough.

I can hear the strain in his voice, the way he's trying to hold it together. The pain begins to ebb, and then something primal takes over as Marius begins to move slowly inside of me. I can feel the sensation of wetness between my legs.

"Good girl," he murmurs. "When a female

accepts a knot, she produces something called slick, which is your way of accepting this physical bond," he says.

My core tightens when I think about it, and I feel my pussy feather around his shaft.

"I'm not going to last long," he continues, moving slowly.

"Me either," I gasp, those tendrils of pleasure making my toes curl. My core clenches as Marius growls, shoving himself deeper inside of me. I can feel his cock pulse inside of me, can feel the way it bobs and thickens, ensuring he won't be able to pull out soon. A week ago, I would've found that thought horrifying, but now? The idea of him being locked inside of me... it makes me cry out as he drives into me, hitting my cervix and causing the bed to creak. I feel wild, primal, like my body recognizes what he is to me.

"Come for me. Crimson," he growls. "I want to feel your pussy milk my cock. I want to see my seed drip out of you, down the inside of your thighs so that I can lick it up and clean you," he adds, grabbing my flesh and pulling me so that he's inside of me to the hilt of his cock. I contract around him at his words, and then a white-hot sensation floods me, and I cry out, seeing stars as my orgasm begins to crest.

"Marius, I'm—" My words are cut off, and I gasp as his cock expands even further, stretching me to an unimaginable amount. *Knotting me.* He doesn't let go as wave after explosive wave hits me, and I can feel his cock curve slightly as he begins to come.

It spurs my orgasm on, extending it as spurt after spurt of his seed hits my cervix. My pussy produces more slick, and the sound it makes causes me to groan with satisfaction. His brutal strength as he drives into me, the last of his come shooting into me, makes me growl—a sound I don't think I've ever made until now. I back my ass up against him, but when he finishes, he holds me still.

"More," I beg, suddenly feeling insatiable.

Marius is breathing heavily behind me, and I hear him chuckle. "This is normal," he murmurs, running a finger down my spine. It causes me to shudder, but he doesn't move his cock from inside of me. *Because he can't*, I think. "And I promise, once my knotting is done, we can go again. We can go all night," he adds, pushing me down so that my stomach is on the bed. He moves his body over me, and still, his cock doesn't move. "It could take a few minutes. It ensures my seed is inside of you, so that we can produce heirs."

I stiffen. Marriage, sure. I reluctantly agreed to that. But a baby? He must sense the change in my mood, because I hear him laugh behind me.

"Only if you want an heir," he adds. "I can turn off my contraceptive power at any time."

"Oh, right," I say softly, resting the side of my face on the cool duvet. My pussy is still throbbing, and my whole body feels like it just got electrocuted. "I should've confirmed all of that before we—"

He nuzzles his mouth into my neck, biting me gently. I shudder at the feel of his teeth on my skin. "When you're ready, I'll pump you full of my seed, Elizabeth," he says. The thought of gushing with his semen causes me to tighten around him, and he laughs. "One day, Crimson.

I want a life with you. I don't have you for very long, so I'm going to ensure I make the most of the time we do have." A wave of sadness rushes through me. He'll live longer than me—and one day, I will die, old and aged while he continues his tour of immortality. I already know I won't want to leave him.

"Or," he purrs, running a finger down the side of my body, "I find a way to join you in the afterworld, so that we can be together forever."

I snort. "Fuck that. Find a way to make me immortal, because I want to see the world with you, Marius. I want to see it all." At those words, I feel his cock come out of me, and his come seeps out immediately. I turn over to face him, pulling his face to mine. "Promise me," I whisper. "Promise me you'll find a way to make me live forever."

His red eyes look down at me, and I swear, they glisten with unshed tears. "I promise. And Elizabeth?"

I look up at him, knowing how vulnerable I am with him, how much I trust him and know he won't hurt me.

"Yes?"

"I do worry about you," he says softly. "I have from the moment I first laid eyes on you." I tilt my head, my eyes narrowing with confusion. And then it hits me. The mirror. *I wish I had someone to worry about me.* I'd uttered those words, and he'd answered. "I wasn't lying when I said I tore the world apart to find you, Crimson. I was going crazy for eighteen years trying to find you," he adds, his voice rich and smooth. A single tear slips down my cheek. "You were never alone, because I've been searching for you."

Without another word, he sheathes himself inside of me, and I groan as he hardens again.

"Marius, I…" I trail off, feeling emotional and powerful all at once. The bond between us… it makes my throat constrict. He puts one leg over his shoulder, and the feeling of his large cock hitting the perfect spot inside of me is overpowering, and I begin to tremble.

"Say it," he growls, slamming into me. A piece of dark hair falls onto his forehead, and he bares his teeth as he rolls his hips on top of me. *Holy Gods.* "Say it, Elizabeth." I moan as his thumb comes down to my clit, circling it around my bud, using my slick as lube.

"I love you, Marius," I say, my voice thick with emotion. I don't know if it's because he's able to pull earth-shattering orgasms out of me, because he found me when I was at my lowest, or because we're fated mates—but whatever the reason, I am beyond grateful for him.

"I love you, too," he answers, and a seismic orgasm rips through us both at the same time. I claw at his back as my body convulses underneath him, and together, we both tumble into wedded, mated bliss.

Thank you for reading Blood & Vows! I hoped you enjoyed Elizabeth and Marius's story. I do plan to expand their story into two full-length books in 2023, **so be sure you're signed up for my newsletter!** I will be sharing that news with my subscribers first.

If you enjoy paranormal romance, I have a rejected mates, wolf-shifter romance trilogy releasing in the fall of 2022! **You can check it out here Shadow Pack Series (I also have the first six chapters available FOR FREE!) Smoke & Shadow**

About
THE AUTHOR

Kory (K.) Easton is the paranormal romance pen name for Amazon bestselling author, Amanda Richardson. She gravitates toward dark tales of otherworldly creatures and beasts. She currently resides in Yorkshire, England, with her husband and two kids.

You can visit my website here:
www.authoramandarichardson.com

Facebook Reader Group:
K. Easton's Kinfolk

For news and updates
please sign up for my newsletter here!

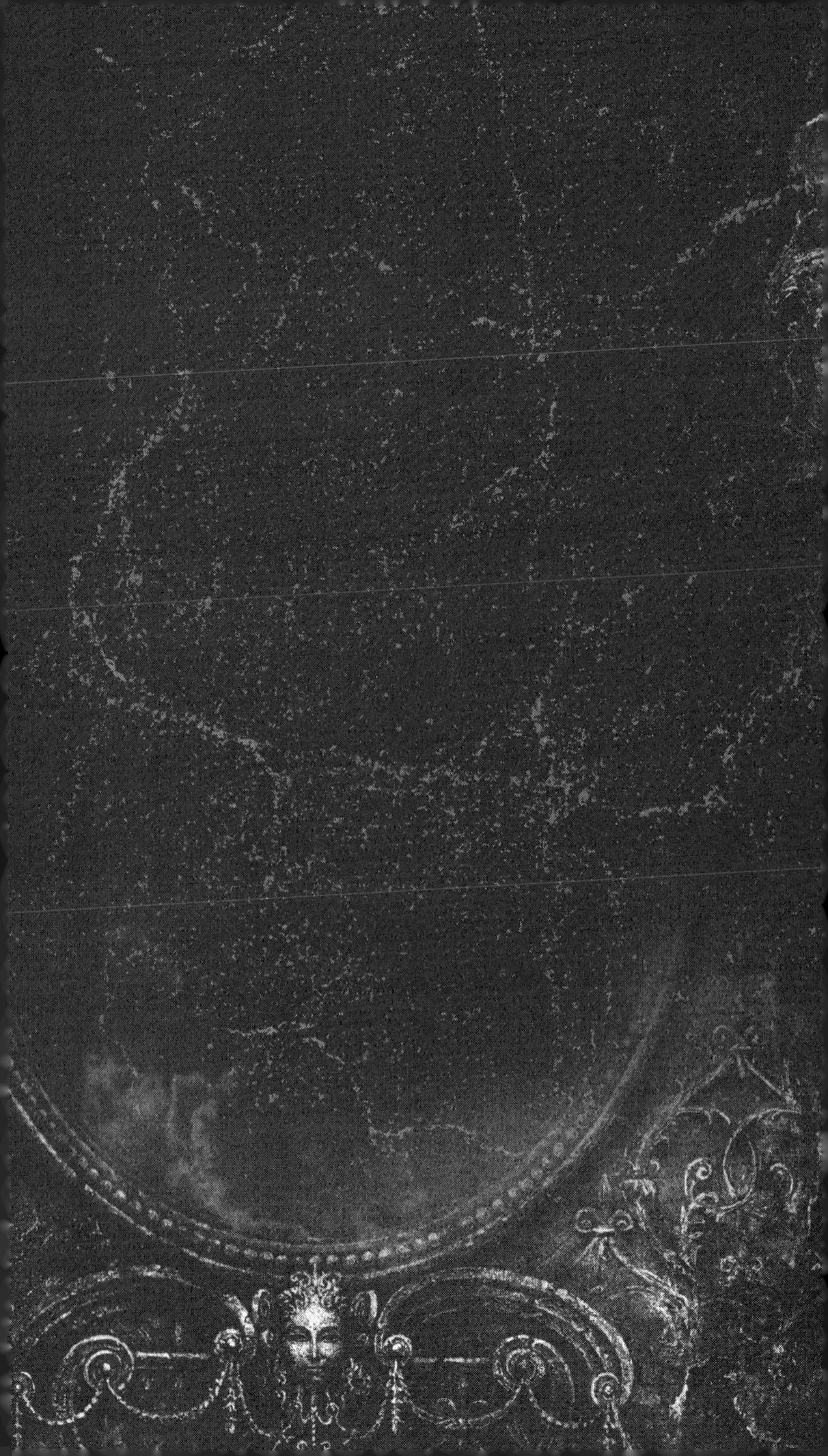

Also by AMANDA RICHARDSON

Love at Work Series
Between the Pages
A Love Like That
Tracing the Stars
Say You Hate Me

HEATHENS Series (Dark Romance)
SINNERS
HEATHENS
MONSTERS
VILLAINS (coming 2023)

Standalones:

The Realm of You
The Island
Dirty Doctor

Ruthless Royals Duet (Reverse Harem)
Ruthless Crown
Ruthless Queen

Savage Hearts Series (Reverse Harem)
Savage Hate
Savage Gods
Savage Reign

Also by
K. EASTON

Shadow Pack Series
(Paranormal Romance, by K. Easton)
Shadow Wolf
Shadow Bride
Shadow Queen

Standalones (K. Easton)
Blood & Vows

Printed in Great Britain
by Amazon